T0194939

PALADIN DUOS

RICHARD M BELOIN MD

authorHOUSE®

AuthorHouse™
1663 Liberty Drive
Bloomington, IN 47403
www.authorhouse.com
Phone: 1 (800) 839-8640

Published by AuthorHouse 06/17/2019

ISBN: 978-1-7283-1593-5 (sc)
ISBN: 978-1-7283-1609-3 (e)

CONTENTS

BOOK 4: MCWAIN ENTERPRISES

DEDICATION

This book is dedicated to all my women readers who have been waiting for the heroine to excel as a bounty hunter and as a business entrepreneur.

BOOK ONE

AMY

CHAPTER 1

AMY'S FORMATIVE YEARS

The sky was blue, the fields were green, and cattle ranching was at its best. But that was not to be the future of one determined eleven year-old girl. Aimee Boudreau, daughter of Romeo Boudreau and Susie Wang, was the third generation of French/Chinese immigrants from Southern Quebec. Romeo and now Suzanne had learned English the hard way from the ranch cowhands, merchants and neighbors. After a lifetime in Texas they still had a slight French/Chinese accent with a twist of Texas drawl!

Aimee's first modernization attempt was

registering at school at age six. She registered as Amy. When she got home, she asked her parents why she had been given the name of Aimee?

Mom answered, "We had never been blessed with children until I was forty-seven. Your dad and I were so happy to have you and we fell in love with you. Your dad kept calling you 'beloved.' When I looked up the meaning in relation to a personal name, it meant 'Aimee.'"

"Well that makes sense, but in Texas, that won't do. From now on my name is Amy and my teacher suggests that we start speaking only English at home if I don't want to fall behind the other kids. Besides, this will help your English as well. We are French and will always have a French/Chinese culture and language, but we live in Texas where people speak English and some Spanish especially on the US/Mexico border. School will be in English with a half hour of Spanish each day."

Amy loved school and excelled in every subject. Her English was perfect with no discernible accent. By the age of ten, her love of homemaking was evident. She was learning to cook, canning the garden vegetables and even bake pastries. She quickly developed the hobby of sewing and because of Amy's interest, Romeo came home with a Singer sewing machine.

By the age of fourteen, Amy found another hobby—shooting guns. Amy convinced an older cowhand, who was known to once have been a gunfighter, to teach her how to shoot a rifle and a pistol. She bought a colt pistol and a Winchester 73 rifle—both in the same caliber, 44-40. She paid for them by sewing clothing for sale. It was a given, that any holiday which included gifts, would always include ammunition.

At the age of sixteen, Amy graduated from grade ten. The town council had been looking for a teacher's assistant for some time. When the teacher recommended Amy, the council offered Amy a part-time job from 8AM to Noon five days a week at a pay of 50 cents a day. The $2.50 was spent on ammo, but that was not enough.

Amy struck a deal with James Westland at the Westland Gun Shop. Amy was allowed to bring a reloader, lead, gunpowder, and primers to her family home. The deal was that Mr. Westland would supply the reloading components and get half of the reloaded ammo for sale. Amy would get the other half as pay for her labor.

With a job, a reloading hobby, shooting practice and sewing, Amy had no time for the social graces. One day, the dilemma for Romeo and Suzanne was exclaimed by Romeo. "what do we do with a rancher's daughter who wants nothing to do with cattle and land, but wants to keep house, cook, teach school, spend hours reloading, shoot guns and sew?"

Suzanne added, "and is not showing any interest in men. I think we need to provide her a trade in case she does not marry and will need to support herself. With her love of sewing, why don't we set her up with a saddlery shop?

"That's a fantastic idea, but first we need to get her trained in the trade. First, let me see Harvey Samuel in his saddlery shop and I'll make him an offer he can't refuse."

A few days later, while Romeo was in town running errands, he stopped at Harvey's shop. Upon entering, the smell of leather was overwhelming. Harvey had just burned someone's name in a holster's backing, and this added to odors. Harvey was presently sewing a section of new harness, and the projects that were ongoing included: a saddle, saddlebags, holsters, scabbards and an assortment of unknown items.

"Good morning Harvey, how is business?"

"Well with the railroad coming to town, the entire settlement is growing by the week. I'm now behind a month in orders and I need help. No one wants to learn the leatherworks trade. My problem is the interruptions from shoppers who are just looking around. If I don't follow them, they rob me blind. I need someone who can handle the cash register, deal with customers, handle the books and help me when there are no customers in the shop."

"Well, what do you have for tools of the trade?"

"I have a boot/shoe sewing machine, a special harness sewing machine, a punch press, a snap/concho applicator, a leather cutting machine, a leather burning kit and too many hand tools to mention."

"I have a deal for you. My daughter is an expert on the Singer sewing machine. She needs to learn a trade. If you were to take her on, she can handle all your business issues. I'm sure she would work out as a leatherworks apprentice. If you take her on, and she accepts, I will pay half of her salary for the next six months as part of an educational fee."

"Wow, I have nothing to lose. I've been advertising the job at $1.25 a day without room and board. I know Amy well, if she had a similar arrangement with James Westland's Gun Shop, we could split her days. I'm certain she would work out."

"This is the ideal time. She works half days as the teacher's helper, but school will be out in one week and Amy will be available full time after the school closing."

During the week Amy had a long talk with her parents. Suzanne started, "Amy, you're now seventeen and within a short year you will be of age. Since you have no present suitors, it's time to think of a profession that can support you now or even after you marry. Right now, you have teaching as an option but that will require sending you off for one year in an approved teaching program. To me sewing is not enough to support you, it is a supplemental form of income. Do you have any other interests in mind?"

"First, teaching and sewing are not to be my future. Mr. Westland has asked me to take an apprentice position in his gun shop. What do you think?"

Romeo lit up, "that's great, gunsmithing is certainly a trade to last another hundred years. What about learning a leatherworks trade?"

"Yes, I love sewing and I suspect I'd also like working with leather. Plus, the two trades supplement each other. I wonder if Mr. Samuel has a spot available?"

"Well, I was in town a few days ago and happened to see a 'help wanted' sign in his window. I think you need to head to town in the morning and talk to both these business men and see if you can become an apprentice in both businesses!"

The next morning, Amy came downstairs all dressed and ready to travel to town. Romeo took one look at his daughter and nearly choked on his oatmeal. Amy was wearing dark blue riding pants with a white blouse and a white cowboy hat. Topped with a medium grey vest and a blue necklace. Her cowboy boots were recently polished, and her clothes did nothing to hide some of her natural curves.

Romeo was speechless and looked at his wife who said, "Amy you look great. Thank goodness you are not wearing your schoolmarm flared dress. I also think you should add your pistol, since everyone in town knows you always wear it—except in school."

As Amy was getting on her horse, she added, "thank you for allowing me to choose my future. Now I have to convince two men that a single female is what they want and need as an apprentice."

***

Amy arrived in town at lunch time since she knew that both businesses closed for an hour at lunch. She then invited both men into the saddlery shop and Amy proceeded to explain that she was applying for a job and why she would fit in as an apprentice.

"I propose to work half days for each of you to make it a full six-day work week. I can handle customers, the cash register, cleaning guns and leather, selling guns and leather goods and take care of your books. In return, you would teach me how to repair guns and do action jobs, as well as sewing leather and all the other crafting techniques needed. I will give you 110% of my effort and you can count on me to be on time and secure with your money. Give me a six-week trial, if I don't pass mustard, then let me go. Do you have any questions?"

Harvey asked, "do you think you can handle heavy harnesses and handle the fine details of leather burning" "Yes, and I'm good at designing patterns for purses, holsters and saddles.

James added, "are you planning to marry and get pregnant?"

"Hey James, I don't think we have the right to ask such personal questions!"

"It's OK, yes I hope to marry some day and have a large family. Assuming I still live in town, I would continue my apprentice. I won't leave you in a lurch if it's in my power to continue my commitment."

Harvey asked, "can we bring up the subject of work dress code?"

"Of course."

"Wear dark clothing since you'll be working with oil, grease and gun powder. Wear a hickory shirt (blue pin stripes with a grey background) or the like. Don't wear a dress. Wear ladies' dark pants such as denim britches. Use the shop aprons and gloves freely."

James took over. "I think it's time to make you a salary offer. The going wage for a cowboy is $1.25 per day including room, board and unlimited ammunition. I would be willing to offer you 75 cents for a half day but six days a week. This also includes a paid lunch at one of our diners. I am certain Harvey will match my offer. In addition, we would pay your livery fees to house your horse."

"That's a great offer and I accept."

Harvey asks, "how do we decide who gets morning or afternoon help?"

Amy answered, "I would alternate each day so that one shop would get me in the morning one day and the afternoon the next day. If the need changes, we can always amend the schedule."

James looked at Harvey and said, "Amy, do you have any questions?"

"Yes, I see that you wear a pistol while in your gun shop. Do you wish me to do the same?"

James said, "yes, I will give you your own Webley Bulldog to wear on your belt like I do. Remember, it is for your self defense and for preventing robberies by intimidation—not for shooting would be robbers. If anyone points a gun at you and demands money, just open the cash register and give it to them. Never put your life in danger just to save a few dollars."

Harvey added, "I agree with James, plus in my shop you can wear a gun if you wish. As a woman, if you feel threatened dealing with male customers, then I understand why wearing a gun can equalize things."

Amy added, "I realize that closing time is 5PM. I fully accept the fact that some extenuating circumstances can occur, and I would be happy to stay and help out. I only ask to travel the three miles to home before dark."

"My next question regards books. Where do I get books on the trade of gun repair and leatherworks?"

"We both have these books in our shops. You can borrow them, and you may even have Mr. Harper order you own copies."

"Before we close, how do you feel working with a young single female?"

"Speaking for Harvey and myself, we both have stable marriages and families. The old biddies, holier than thou and gossip mongers don't come in our shops. If trouble comes our way, I think we would be able to deal with it."

James closed the interview by saying, "you're hired, when can you start working?"

"Tomorrow morning, today I need to go

to Harper's Mercantile and buy a new work wardrobe!"

Harvey adds, "take three different outfits and put them on my tab."

To match Harvey's gesture, James hands Amy her Webley Bulldog with a belt/holster and a box of 44 rimfire ammo.

***

CHAPTER 2

THE APPRENTICE YEAR

Monday morning, Amy was sitting on the boardwalk enjoying her cup of coffee from Suzie's Diner. At 8AM James arrived to unlock his shop and found a smiling Amy sitting on the boardwalk. To start the day, James decided to give Amy a tour of the shop.

"Here is your key to the front door. Let's start with your shop opening and closing procedure. Keeping the closed sign in the window, slide this steel bar to lock the door. Open the Mosler safe using the combination 60-17-53. Remove the dozen new rifles, and new pistols. Place them in the display case. Bring the cash tray and place it in the register. Then you turn the sign to open and unlock the door. Closing is simply the reverse plus lock the safe with a right-hand spin."

"Let's review the gun sales. The new pistol prices are based on the delivered invoice price plus 10%. These prices are firm. If trading firearms, I'll have to give you a trade value. The holsters are from Harvey and the prices also reflect a 10% profit. The new rifle and shotgun prices are also labeled and firm. With used firearms you can negotiate a price, but never lower the price more than 10%. When buying a used gun, offer the customer 60% of the replacement value if the firearm is in good condition. With the current black powder, never take in a used gun without viewing the bore's condition. Keep your invoices and price lists handy and never hesitate to refer to them before making a deal. If in doubt, ask me. Most important, never hesitate to ask me any question—that's how you'll learn, heh?"

"Note that our big pistol seller is the Colt 1873 Peacemaker in 45 Colt but is available in other calibers. It comes in different barrel lengths to include: the 3-inch Sheriff's Model, the 4 ¾ inch gunfighter model, the standard 5 ½ inch model, the 7 ½ inch military model, and the 12-inch Buntline model. The competition to the Colt is the Smith and Wesson Model 3 in 44 rimfire or 45 Schofield calibers. This pistol only comes with a 6 ½ inch barrel. Depending on accessories, the selling prices are comparable."

"Is there an advantage between the Colt and the Smith and Wesson?"

"The appreciable difference is between loading and unloading. The Smith and Wesson is a break open pistol which ejects all six rounds simultaneously and reloading is quicker since the cylinder is completely exposed. The Colt is a single eject and reloading. Other than that, the feel and look of the gun becomes a personal preference."

"What are these different pistols?"

"Those are the new Model 1877 double action pistols made by Colt. The Thunderer in 41 caliber and the Lightning in 38 caliber. They are more expensive and still slow sellers."

"One last thought, whenever you sell a firearm, old or new, always give them a receipt with the gun's model and serial number, and the date of purchase."

"Moving on are the three last tables and one display. The first is the gun cleaning table which you already know. The second table is the action job table and the third table is the gun repair table—we'll come back to these later. Note that all three tables face the customers, that keeps your eyes on customers with sticky fingers. The last display is the ammo and accessories table."

"Monday is my slow day. So, today your job is to dismantle a Colt Peacemaker and reassemble it—and repeat, repeat and repeat. I will do the first and show you how to follow my stepwise procedure for both dismantling and reassembly." James was able to do both maneuvers in ten minutes.

"Wow, you've pulled out some twenty small parts, and reassembled them, and you expect me to do the same?" James nodded yes with a smile.

"Ok, here goes nothing." Amy worked hard

and needed help in one reassembly step, even if she was following his stepwise sequence. The first attempt took her 45 minutes. By noon she was getting the knack of it and completed the last attempt in 25 minutes. When ready to move on to Harvey's, she said, "I'm going to practice on my own Colt tonight and tomorrow I'll be able to approach your time, heh!"

During the lunch hour, James went to run errands and Amy stayed in the locked shop to check out the different books James had on the shelves. Amy wrote down the names of the books she would want to purchase for herself. By 1PM she stepped next door to Harvey's.

Harvey was an organized leather man. As Amy walked in, he said, "God, I'm glad you're here and here is your key. Let me say that I make holsters/gunbelts and harnesses. That's all the time I have and I'm way behind. I no longer make saddles or saddlebags since Harper can order them cheaper thru Montgomery Ward than I can make them."

"As your introductory tour, lets talk about leather. I buy my leather as tanned hides ready for use. Leather thickness is measured in ounces. One-ounce leather is equal to 1/64th inch. I use 4-ounce leather or 4/64 = 1/16th of an inch for holsters and 8-ounce leather or 8/64 = 1/8th inch for harnesses. For holsters, I can double the layers for holding its shape. For harnesses I can double or triple layers to match the strength needed to handle the load."

"Standing in the shop I see tools, but where is your leather inventory?"

"Open that back door. The shelves on the left is 4-ounce and on the right is 8-ounce leather."

Amy opens the door and gets an unaccustomed potent whiff of leather, as she turns and smiles at Harvey.

"To finish my tour, this table has the hardware we'll be using: The most often used is a complete assortment of rivets. Plus, O-rings, buckles, D-rings, loops, snaps, fasteners, Conchos, Chicago screws, grommets, eyelets, button studs and more."

"This next table is hand tools. The most frequently used are punches. Others include stamps, mallets, scissors, round knife, blades, bevellers, carving knives, awls and many more."

"Machinery includes the master sewing machine, power cutter, punch press, rivet setter and many more. All machinery is run by using foot power—just like your Singer sewing machine."

"Before we get to harnesses, let's talk about holsters and gun-belts. I have two grades of holsters, fancy with tooled or burnished leather, and economy. Both come with a choice of single or double ply 4 or 8-ounce thickness. The leather color comes in brown, black or burgundy. The holster types include Buscadero, high riding Mexican loop, cross draw and backpack. The buckling types include the Ranger belt and the Tapered Tongue End belt. Accessories include belt loops for pistol/rifle ammo or shotgun shells. We'll be working on these after the harness orders are all caught up."

"The last portion of my tour is this masterpiece. I have laid out a real harness on these benches. I did this to show you the basic parts of a standard harness. The first part and the most important is the neck collar or 'hames' as it's called. This part I purchase from a factory and I keep at least eight different sizes and three of each. Some are light duty, but most are heavy duty. I faithfully maintain my inventory thru telegraph orders to the factory."

"Now the other harness pieces include: breast plate, belly band, saddle strap, back strap, loin strap and the breeching strap. Plus, a few other minor straps. This is the portion we manufacture out of leather hides. For the next ten days, we'll be making harnesses. If you are ready, let's build a harness for a large gelding pulling a standard family buckboard."

Harvey showed Amy how to operate the power cutter to make straight strips or straps with squared-off ends. Harvey brought the gelding close to the shop and was giving Amy exact measurements for individual pieces. While Amy was cutting, Harvey was punching the ends and fitting/crimping rivets to attach the round and square rings between pieces. When Amy got ahead of Harvey, he showed her how to use the punch press to help him along.

By 5PM, the harness was complete in every detail, and a perfect fit. Harvey said, "I can't believe this, we started the harness at 2PM and we are done in three hours. When I worked alone, this size harness would have taken me two full days."

"Remember the old adage, 'a man working alone will take three days on a project, whereas, two men working together will do the same project in one day'—saving the employer a full day's wages, heh!"

"I'll make a deal with you. To help you catch up on back orders, spend some time tonight pre-cutting all the straps we'll need for tomorrow's job. I'll be here to start an hour early and we can use the lunch hour to finish the job if necessary. I know you have a pair of large Percherons in the back barn, but from 7AM-1PM we'll get the job done and I won't charge you any extra wages."

"How can I say no, see you at 7AM."

That evening before going home, Amy went to Harper's Mercantile and ordered four books—repairing firearms to include Colt

Peacemakers, Smith and Wesson Model 3, Winchester 73's, and Remington double barrel shotguns.

At home, after dinner and clean up, Amy practiced dismantling and reassembly until it all became second nature to her. The first time she dismantled the gun, Romeo and Suzanne were totally astonished to see the gun torn down to 20 or more pieces. They were skeptical that this thing could be put back together and still fire. Amy shocked both as she reassembled the gun in six minutes, placed one round in the cylinder, and stepped outside to shoot off the live round.

Amy arrived at 6:30 and Harvey was already at work. The pair of Percherons were tied to the rear hitching rail and a table had several piles of pre-cut straps with different widths. Harvey handed Amy a cup of fresh coffee and said, "I'm ready to start."

The team went to work. Amy was using the punch press and Harvey was using the rivet setter. Pieces with different rings were attached and draped over the Percheron upon completion. Watching Harvey measure and design the final product, Amy realized that Harvey was a master craftsman. Amy smiled as she realized that she would learn so much from this man.

The new thing with this heavy-duty harness was the doubling or two-ply straps. These were sewn together. Amy immediately caught on how to run the leather sewing machine, and Harvey let her sew the two-ply pieces.

By mid-morning the first harness was completed. As they were about to take a quick coffee break, Harvey's wife, Natalie came in the shop with a basket of freshly baked cookies. Natalie said, "I can't believe you have one of those large harnesses completed by now, and it looks great. Didn't I tell you 'get some help months ago.'"

"Yes dear, now thanks for the cookies but we have to get back to work to complete the second harness before 1PM."

To help train Amy, on this harness, Amy was using the rivet setter and Harvey was using the punch press. When Amy got the gist of this tool, the tempo picked up and they applied the last connecting strap at 12:30PM. As they were both admiring their work, a farmer arrived on horseback. He stepped down and kept staring at the two Percherons with the new harnesses. "Yes Amos, those are your Percherons with the new harnesses."

"Now that is a fine job. I was coming to see you to offer you more money to get these harnesses within a few days since my other team needs to rest a while. I've been over working them."

"The price is the same, $30 apiece."

"Here is a bank voucher for $70. I'll trail these two with a long rope and they're coming home wearing their new harnesses. Thanks Harvey."

As Amy was leaving for the gun shop, Harvey yells out, "catch." Coming at her were two silver dollars in midair. Catching them and realizing what she had in her hand, Harvey adds, "that's a tip for the extra help and a lot of motivation energy, heh!"

That afternoon, James had her afternoon planned. After watching her dismantle and reassemble a Colt in ten minutes, he moved on to the next instruction. "Today I'm going to show you how to perform an action job on a Colt pistol. James and Amy each had their own new and dismantled Colt laid out. James showed her how to use a fine India stone to file off burrs or very rough areas on the internal parts and the gun frame. Afterwards, each part was buffed with a 400-grit metal sand- paper, followed by 800-grit and finishing with 1200-grit. After cleaning off the metallic dust, the gun was reassembled—some two hours later.

James adds, "Now pull and release the hammer on a new Colt with and without an action job."

"Wow, it's like day and night. Why would anyone not want one with an action job?"

"For two reasons, one is the extra $4 charge and the second is the belief that use will smooth it out. What they don't realize is that it takes 1000 rounds to smooth out an action compared to a $4 action job. For now, this is the productive activity that you can do between serving customers. Just as I spend my time repairing guns. Later, you'll also learn gun repair."

The remainder of the day was spent serving customers. James was kept busy receiving broken guns and Amy had several sales. During the afternoon, Amy managed to perform a second action job between customers. Just before closing James dismantled and reassembled a Winchester 73. This was simpler than a Colt pistol but would require some practice at home tonight. As she was leaving, James added, "in the future, I'll show you the disassembly and reassembly of a Remington shotgun and a Smith and Wesson Model 3. Once you have these four guns mastered and learned the proper action jobs for each gun, you'll be ready to start repairing them."

Over the next week two things happened. Harvey caught up his harness back orders, and James was done with dismantling/reassembly and action job instructions. Time arrived to be exposed to repairing guns and crafting holsters, gun-belts and scabbards.

"Repairing guns is simple, "look how the gun is not properly functioning, then dismantle it. Look at all the parts. Find the broken part, or worn part, or bent pin, or broken spring, or weak spring, or broken screw, or missing part such as a pin that fell out. If you know your internal parts, you can tell where the problem is."

"The rule about repairing guns is to determine for the customer whether it's worth repairing the gun. If the cost of replacing parts and labor is still less than the value of the gun, repair it. If it's greater, it's time to retire the firearm. Your customer needs to know and agree to this before he leaves the firearm in your hands."

Amy loved the challenge of a broken gun. James saw early on that she had the ability to quickly find the culprit in a broken gun. The customers quickly realized how pleasant it was to be served by a polite young lady who was very knowledgeable about her firearms.

James business had doubled, and he finally was able to take days off. After two months, he gave Amy a raise to $1.25 per half day. On days that he took off he added 5% of the daily take to her wages.

There was some drive about the leather

shop that Amy could not understand until she started working on holsters. Harvey started the day with this line, "today we are beginning holster, gunbelts, and scabbards. We will make five holsters of each kind and I expect you to make the fifth one of each type. The sequence will be economical-Mexican loop-single ply cross draw-double ply cross draw, Buscadero, backpack, scabbards, Buscadero belts, ranger belts and tapered tongue end belts. On second thought, I will also add pommel holsters."

"What is a pommel holster?"

"That's an economical single ply holster without a belt loop. Instead, the holster is attached to a flat apron which has a hole in the top to fit over the saddle horn. It makes for comfortable riding without a gunbelt that is usually stored in the saddlebags. The pistol is easily accessed if needed."

Harvey started looking for a pattern that would fit a Colt with a 4 ¾ inch barrel. He then traced the pattern onto a 4-ounce piece of pre-dyed top grain leather, leather that had been sanded to level high fibers. After using a combination of knives and blades to cut the pattern out, he then placed the piece of leather thru a leather softening process with hot water. Then the master went to work bending the leather into a holster, sewing the edges and forming a belt loop. The final product was oiled to a bright and smooth finish.

Amy did the next four with Harvey directing and helping her out. By the fifth one, Harvey watched her without touching or talking. At the end Amy broke out in a smile as she handed Harvey the finished product. Harvey examined the holster and said, "goodness, this is a nice piece, actually a better holster than mine."

Moving on thru the remainder of the holsters, Harvey followed the routine: do one, teach one, help with one, and let Amy do the fourth. Amy's favorite one was the Buscadero holster. It was harder to mold two layers and had a longer loop to the Buscadero belt. But it allowed Amy's creative talent to show thru carving, tooling, edging and burnishing of the surface layer.

Having mastered all the holsters, all she

needed was more practice to improve the product's quality from experience. The three belts proved easy compared to holsters. The power cutter would cut the strips. There was some shaping and angle contouring to the Buscadero belt, but the ranger and tapered tongue were straight belts with a either a straight or tapered tongue. The buckles were the universal other end of the belt. Sewing ammo loops was an easy accessory to add.

Scabbards were simply a single ply extra long holster with a lot of sewing. It also had several small straps to attach the scabbard to the saddle. The patterns used produced scabbards for a Winchester 73 carbine or rifle, and for a standard barrel shotgun or coach shotgun. Any other firearm would require a special order.

After several days of instruction, Amy said, "you forgot to show me how to make a shotgun backpack holster."

"That holster has to be made by special order for three reasons. First, it has to match the model of shotgun. Second, it has to match the barrel length and third, the shoulder straps have to match the size of the carrier and body habitus. When I get an order, I'll be sure to show you how to measure the customer for a perfect fit. Then I will show you how to build one of these holsters."

At the closing of three days working on these products, Harvey went over the price list. "I charge according to cost of materials, plus labor. Special orders get a 10% surcharge tacked on. James gets a 10% discount with volume orders."

Basic Mexican loop	$5
Cross draw-single ply	$5
Cross draw-2 ply	$9
Buscadero	$12
Pommel	$6
Ranger or tapered belt	$5
Buscadero belt	$7
Belt loops	$2
Short scabbard	$11
Long scabbard	$13

It was Amy who realized the key to making holsters and scabbards, it was the pattern.

With the correct pattern for a known firearm, the finished product was likely to fit the gun. Realizing this she asked, "what do you do when you get a special order for a holster or scabbard that you don't have the pattern?"

"You take the gun and try to insert it in the pre made holsters. See where it binds or is loose and fit it for length. It's a hit or miss system, but with experience, you'll get good at it. This is one that I will help you with."

Over the months Harvey's routine had completely changed. Instead of always being behind with his orders, he now could deliver a single harness in one day and a double in two days. He finally built a reserve of gunbelts, holsters and scabbards. He always wanted to add a new holster that would fit "all purposes" and he asked Amy to design it.

The next day she came back with a pattern that was traceable. They made one to reveal that it was a cross between a 2-ply cross draw, a Mexican loop and a Buscadero. It was a 2-ply molded holster to a specific pistol with an apron backing and a two-inch drop below the belt—not the extreme drop of a Buscadero rig.

The word quickly got around and Harvey and Amy were working overtime just to keep up with the orders. It was at that time that Harvey increased Amy's wages to $1.25 for a half day. He also gave her 10% of the sales for the new holster she had designed.

Over the weeks to follow, Amy got comfortable with her new professions. She read every book from the shop and her own purchases. She was building her own library. She enjoyed every day and found something new to learn on a daily basis.

Amarillo was a quiet town, but one day the unlikely event happened despite the fact that the gun shop was next door to Harvey and on the other side with the sheriff's office. A scruffy individual came in and stepped up to the gun repair table as Amy was working with a customer at the sales display. Suddenly, the man pulled a pistol, pointed it at James and demanded his cash in the register.

Amy looked left, saw that the pistol's hammer

was still down and in a reflexive moment pulled her Bulldog and shot the robber's pistol out of his hand. The gunshot brought Harvey and Sheriff Gusfield running in with guns drawn. Sheriff Gusfield looked at the situation and said, "well Amy, I had heard rumors that you had become a crack shot, guess they are true. Now Sam Weber, why did you do such a foolish thing?"

"Desperation, I guess. With the drought, I haven't been able to bring in a crop and the wife and kids are hungry. As soon as I pulled the gun out, I knew it was a mistake, but it was already too late. Guess Amy's shot saved me from actually succeeding as an armed thief."

As Sheriff was getting the facts from Amy, James picked up Sam's pistol, checked it out and straightened the cylinder pin which had been bent by the bullet's impact. James finally spoke up. "Here is your gun back and I repaired it. Also, I won't be filing any charges. Next time you need money, just ask me as he hands Sam a twenty-dollar bill."

When Amy saw the money being given, she

had her first epiphany as an approaching adult. She instinctively reached in her pocket and pulled out a 20-dollar double eagle and handed it to Sam. "Sorry for shooting at you."

Sam was flabbergasted. He looked at the $40 dollars and started to tear up. Sheriff Gusfield piped up and said, "here, here now, a man pride is all he has along with his family. So, leave with your chin up and go take care of your family. Maybe someday, you can do a favor for someone else."

Once the shop was empty, Harvey asked why she had given away an entire week's pay. "Because, for the first time in my life, I did something that made me feel good. One of these days, I'll be in a position to do more for the needy with my money."

Amy spots something out of Harvey's pants pocket and asks what the item was. Harvey answers, "it's your premature 18th birthday gift. Some day you either won't have your Bulldog or you had been disarmed by a miscreant. Pull this out of your pocket and smack the round tip onto an assailant's forehead. This is a ten-inch long double layered strap with a flexible steel rod along its length and a poured lead flat medallion in the round portion. If you snap this on his forehead, he'll collapse to the ground. If you smack him in the knee cap, it will shatter it, and again collapse him to the ground. Now if you smack him in the groin, he'll pass out and wake up with a permanent high-pitched voice, heh."

"Thank you, Harvey, if I ever have to use it, I'll be thinking of you."

During the remainder of the year, there was never an idle moment in Harvey's shop since he was taking holster orders from other gun shops and even harness orders from other saddlery shops in town who preferred to build saddles instead of harnesses. James shop had some slow periods. Amy found a solution to replace dead time with productive time. James ordered some current more efficient reloading equipment, and they started loading 12-gauge shotgun shells in 00 buck, #3 buck and #6 birdshot. They also started loading powerful center fire ammo in 45-70 for the new model Winchester 1876. Other than the rimfire 44 and 22, they eventually reloaded all the center fire calibers that were in the ammo display case—including odd calibers for the Sharps rifle. The only ammo that Amy took home was her pre-arranged 50-50 ratio for the 44-40 ammo—for personal use.

The apprentice year was coming to an end on her 18th birthday, which was a week away. Amy was still spending her evenings reading about gun repairs and leather works when her parents came to talk with her. Her dad started, "anticipating that at 18 you'll likely want to move out and get your own apartment in town, we also have changes coming. Your mom is 65 and I'm 68 years old. It is a miracle we lived this long, but it's time for us to sell the ranch and move into town. Russel next door has been after us to sell out so he can expand his land and herd."

Her mom took over, "He is offering us $5,000 for the six sections of land, $16,000 for 800 head of cattle, and $3,000 for the house, barn, well, bunkhouse, ten horses and several wagons. That, along with our bank life's savings of $26,000 we'll be able to survive with an interest rate of 2.5% yielding $1250 per year. We have made a deposit on a small house in town and would like you to join us until you feel the need to move into your own apartment or house. What do you think?"

"Love it, let's do it before you change your mind."

"No chance, it will likely take two weeks to get everything organized. We'll see Russel tomorrow and go finalize the ranch sale in town."

The next day, it was work as usual at the gun shop. Sheriff Gusfield walked in with some alarming news. "There is a new trend where outlaw gangs are sneaking out of hiding in the Indian Nations. Since we are only 100 miles from the border, we can expect to see them at work"

James asks, "what do you mean by 'at work?'"

"A gang ravages a town, steals supplies, robs banks and then attacks nearby ranches to rob them and cause mayhem. Some ranch houses have been burned, inhabitants beaten or knocked out, and women stolen. Finally, a ranching couple was murdered because they would not open their safe. So far, all four towns north of us to include, Pampa, Borger, Dumas and Dalhart, have been hit hard. These four towns are only fifty miles away and we expect that we are next on their list."

Amy asks, "What can the law do to stop these animals?"

"Those four northern towns had either no lawman or lawmen incapable of stopping them. I have sent for the Texas Rangers, but may not arrive in time to save the ranchers. Hopefully, my presence with three deputies will be enough to keep them out of our town. So meanwhile, my three deputies are out on the trail warning ranchers to be ready and armed at all times."

"Why are they stealing women?"

"To service their men back in the Nations."

James added, "these types of men are psychopaths. They have no respect for human life and feel no remorse in killing human beings. They kill for pleasure, for eliminating witnesses, or for punishing resistant victims."

Amy pauses and says, "then someone has to remove these evil beings from humanity. Now who could do this?"

Sheriff Gusfield says, "either lawmen as their job, or bounty hunters for money."

Amy realized she had just experienced her second epiphany. Her first was the need for someone to help those in financial need. This one was that someone needs to stop these evil animals.

A week later the Burdog Gang was camped some ten miles north of Amarillo. The gang leader, Zeek Burdog was talking to his six men. We're running out of supplies and we're overdue for drinking, poker and women. I think we need to check out Amarillo as our next town and it's surrounding ranches before we head south to Lubbock. So, I'm sending Sam and Rickter as forward scouts. I want you to check out the locations of the banks, saloons, hotels and lawmen offices. To give you some business cover, take the three broken rifles and two frozen pistols to a gun shop and trade them in for some new ones."

A few days later, two men entered the

Westland Gun Shop. Amy was out back unpacking new supplies, so the men stepped up to Jamie. "How can I help you, gents?"

"We have some broken guns we would like to trade for new ones."

"Fine, leave them and come back in one hour and I'll have a value for each one."

After the men left, Jamie starts to check out the guns and calls up Amy to verify his trade value. Amy looks at the barrels, and the mechanisms and says, "James, all these bores are corroded, and no rifling is remaining. The mechanisms are also corroded with powder."

"These guns have never been cleaned. It would cost more to replace the parts than it will cost to buy a new one. These guns have no value as they are."

"You are right, so let's work together to dismantle them and clean them up to see if they have any value."

An hour later the job was done. The mechanisms were at least operational, but the barrels were shot-out. Amy said, "offer them $5 each and we'll sell them for $7 as a short-range self-defense weapon—pistol up to 5 yards and rifle up to 20 yards."

When the men returned, James explained the reason for a low trade value. One of the men was insulted when the trade value was mentioned at $5. He drew his pistol and said, "well in that case, open and empty your cash register as well as put those four new pistols in this burlap bag."

Amy was standing to James right doing an action job. When she realized the gun toting outlaw was gathering cash from James, she yells out, "hey, look at me."

As the smelly, dirty and scruffy animal turned to look at Amy, she pulls her Bulldog and shoots the miscreant's ear off. The impact must have sent a sound wave to his brain, because the outlaw placed his hand to his ear and collapsed. His partner had his hands in the air when the sheriff walked in with his pistol in hand.

The two outlaws were arrested and the one missing his ear had to be carried to jail for medical attention. Once both were locked up, Sheriff Gusfield went thru wanted posters.

He found the two that matched the outlaws—
wanted dead or alive for murder and bank
robbery with a $750 reward on each one.

Later that day, Amy was informed that
she had two $750 vouchers coming from the
Western Union Telegraph. That was Amy's
third epiphany in a few days. *There is money
to be made as a bounty hunter and that allows
the financial support of victims—but a dangerous
profession.*

Over the next two weeks, the freighting
company moved the Boudreaus to the
new house on a quiet street in town. The
homestead had been bought by Russel, and the
Boudreaus were spending their last night at the
homestead awaiting the final freight wagon in
the morning. Amy was reminiscing her years
on the homestead when riders were heard
approaching the homestead. Suddenly the front
door was kicked in and five masked gun toting
men rushed the parlor. Suzanne was knocked
unconscious with a gun tap on the head, Romeo
was gunned to the floor with a shot to the left
shoulder and Amy was subdued with a punch

to the face. The last she remembered were the words of the gang's leader, "tie her up to a horse and we'll enjoy her later. If she gives you too much trouble lay her across her saddle on her belly with her hands and feet tied under the horse's belly—just like a sack of potatoes."

"Ok Pops tell me where your money is or we'll kill your wife. We still have our face masks on, so you can't recognize us. That means, both you and your wife can live another day. Just give me the combination to your safe or your hiding place."

"Since we are in the process of moving, I only have $1,000 in the safe. The combination is 80-21-56. Take it and get out."

After the outlaws left, Romeo tried to get up but slipped and fell on his shot-up shoulder, making him pass out. Suddenly he felt water splashing on his face. As Romeo woke up, he saw a well shaven clean looking young men looking at him who was asking questions.

"Who are you, what happened here, and where is the nearest doctor?"

My name is Romeo Boudreau and we were

robbed by a gang of outlaws. The nearest doctor is in town, three miles away."

"I saw a wagon when I arrived. I'll use it to bring you and your unconscious wife to the doc."

"Wait, before I pass out again, please listen to me. Why did you show up here at this time?"

"I'm a bounty hunter on the trail of a well-known gang the Burdog gang. Their tracks lead me to your house."

"Ok, this gang kidnapped our daughter for nefarious reasons. Hoping you're not too late, bring her back to us alive and I will give you a reward of $10,000. She's our only world."

Realizing something more, Romeo asked, "what is your name?"

"My name is Randy McWain, and I'll bring your daughter back!"

***

BOOK TWO

RANDY

CHAPTER 3

RANDY'S EARLY YEARS

Randy was raised in a medium sized town some 70 miles southeast of Amarillo, on the road to Dallas and along the railroad route. It was a quiet community whose economy was ranching and growing cotton. The railroad with its loading pens for cattle and its loading docks for cotton provided the quick freight to meat processing plants and cotton mills.

Randy was never involved with either of these industries. As a young boy between the ages of six to age twelve, Randy enjoyed playing with his friends. His parents saw a potential problem in raising a child in town—too much time with nothing to do for kids. So, they decided by Randy's twelfth birthday to do something about it. His dad was the vice president of the only local bank and his mom was a records copier at the same bank. To avoid Randy being left alone at home, they got him a job after school and another job during the summer.

His after-school jobs included: delivering papers from one business to another, sweeping the floors at several businesses, and delivering groceries to elderly or shut-ins. His summer job was with the local freighting company. In the morning, the team would pick up the horse manure in all the town streets. In the afternoon, they would unload arriving freighting wagons to the different merchants and outlying ranchers.

Along with working 8—10 hours each summer day, Randy befriended an old bullwhacker who had once been a gunfighter. At the age of 14, Randy had developed an interest in guns and gun handling. With his back wages and a loan from his dad, he bought a new Colt in 44-40, a new Winchester 73 rifle in the same caliber and a used double barrel 12-gauge shotgun.

Randy learned the proper fast draw technique using a Gunfighter rig made for that purpose. To be well rounded, he also learned the proper rifle shooting techniques for quick short-range shots, as well as the 100-yard free-style shooting. With the double barrel shotgun, he learned the proper shucking of spent shells and quick double shell reloading technique.

Earning 50 cents a day was not supporting his shooting needs when loaded ammo was selling for a penny per loaded bullet. Randy recognized that gun proficiency would require large amounts of ammo which he couldn't afford at his pay grade. He went to the local mercantile owned by Omer Schilling. He checked display prices of ammo and Montgomery Ward for state-of-the-art reloading equipment. He then sat outside on the boardwalk and did some serious ciphering. Once he was sure of his figures, he walked in the mercantile to talk to Mr. Schilling.

"Sir, you are getting shafted by your supply

company. They are charging you 45 cents for fifty 45 long colt bullets and you are selling the box of fifty for 50 cents. That's a 10% profit. Now I have the figures here that if I reload five boxes of 50 bullets, that you get three boxes of fifty rounds and I get two boxes. By my computation, with you paying for all the components and tools, you still make a profit of 25% and you didn't have to do anything but put the loaded ammo in your display case."

Omer was impressed with the fourteen-year-old teenager. When Randy left the store, he had a new reloader, bullet mold and all the components to go into business. His dad was not really enthused about Randy and his love of guns but realized that he may have a future as a lawman. For now, being involved in a gainful purpose and a business enterprise at age 14 was a step in the right direction.

Between the ages of 14 to 16, Randy continued his routine of school till 3PM and odd jobs till 7PM dinner at home. Evenings spent practice shooting or reloading. Summers brought him back at the freight line for 50 cents a day till graduation from the 10th grade in the spring of 1980. For the next two years, he worked five days a week at $1 a day.

When Randy reached the legal age of 18, he was made an offer he could not refuse. Sheriff Wilcox said, "Randy I've seen you handle your guns and you are very secure with them; you have a strong work ethic and clear living skills. I think you should consider being my deputy on a trial basis"

Randy looked at the sheriff and said, "yes, I believe I can handle being a deputy and I'm happy to learn from you. When do I start?"

"Tomorrow, show up at 8AM with your guns and trail gear. Put your horse and trail gear in the livery to be paid for by the council. Bring your guns and ammo to the office with your personal clothing and items. You will have your own living quarters in the back office. Your pay will be $45 a month to include meals and unlimited practice ammo. Any arrested outlaw with a reward on his head will be your financial gain. That also allows you to sell his horse, guns and other personal items if the outlaw is sent to prison or executed."

***

Randy arrived at 7:30 with all his gear. Sheriff Wilcox was already making coffee and showed Randy his new home room where he unpacked and put everything away. Sitting down with a cup of coffee, Sheriff Wilcox began, "in the office we use our first names, in the public I'm called Sheriff Wilcox and you're called Deputy McWain. The council pays for our coffee, so always keep a pot going on the coal stove."

"Our job as lawmen is to keep the peace, enforce state and town laws, and do it safely. In face of impossible odds, you're not expected to put your life in danger to do your job. That may sound ridiculous but let me give you two examples. Just because there is a gang of known killers in town, you're not expected to go against them alone. Whereas, if the same gang is trying to rob the bank, it is your job to try to stop them. And so, there is some risk to this job but you're not alone."

"I will spend the next six months with you, from 8AM to 5PM. You will be on your own overnight. As we go thru the daily routines, I will show you the safe ways to do your job. At all times, wear your pistol. When doing rounds or answering a disturbance, wear this backpack with a sawed-off shotgun. The appearance of a lawman with a sawed-off shotgun in hand has a way of defusing a situation without gunfire. There is one ready with a backpack holster at Labor's Gun Shop—a welcome gift from me."

The remainder of the introduction included the swearing in. Randy was given his deputy badge and multiple new employee forms were signed.

"Now let's go on rounds. Walking along the boardwalks, there is always a chance for an ambush from revengeful friends and family of those you arrested. Keep your eyes busy. Look at rooftops for snipers, back-step when moving across an alley, watch out for doors opening after you walk by, look carefully at unknown faces you meet on boardwalks, and don't forget a man on horseback—always be defensive."

"We have a dozen merchants in town and two saloons. Most of our security is spent guarding them from robbery or mayhem, as well as providing law enforcement for the townspeople. The remainder of our time is spent providing law for the ranchers and homesteaders within the town's jurisdiction. Serving papers is the least pleasant aspect of this job."

"Other than that, during the day I like to wave at merchants. If they don't acknowledge me, I know there is a problem. I even stop in the saloons and have a chat with the bartenders. During evening rounds, I check and make sure all doors are locked and lanterns are off.

Although Randy was already well known in town, that first afternoon, they rode in the nearby country side to make introductions to ranchers and homesteaders. Upon return to town, a ruckus was spotted outside the "Wet Bucket Saloon." Two men were at it with fists flying. Sheriff Wilcox said, "There is no way I'm getting into that fight. I'll wait till it's time to stop it. If one pulls a knife, I stop it. If one is beating the pulp out of his opponent, I stop it."

"How do you stop it?"

"I fire a shot in the air and that usually works. Unless there is a significant persistent threat, I don't arrest anyone."

Heading back to the office, Randy asks Sam how he does an alley back-step. Sam shows him how to step across an alley and then step backwards to watch the alley for unwanted visitors who would shoot you in the back.

With the sheriff home, Randy spent the evening reading town and state statutes. At 11PM, he put his backpack shotgun on and went on his rounds. Things seemed quiet till a gunshot rang out. Randy rushed to Wilder's Saloon. Stepping in the batwing doors he drew his shotgun as he saw a man standing by someone on the floor and holding a gun in his hand.

Randy says, "what happened here?" The bartender answered, "two men had an argument over a pot of money. Suddenly, this man stands up, draws his pistol and shoots the other unarmed man in the head."

One of the other men at the table says, "he was armed with a belly gun."

Randy asks the bartender to roll the man over to see if he had a belly gun on him or on the floor. There was none.

Randy asks if anyone else saw what had happened. Several men yelled out that the bartender was right. The dead man was not armed and the man standing shot him in cold blood.

Randy looks at the shooter and says, "drop your gun, put your hands in your back and you're under arrest pending further investigation by Sheriff Wilcox."

"Never happen, sonny." As he holsters his gun, the three other men stood up and the other patrons cleared the area expecting some serious gunplay.

"Me and my three boys are leaving and if you try to stop us, you're a dead man."

"You all put your hands up. If you draw your pistols, you will all get a dose of #3 Buckshot."

In slow motion, Randy saw all four men draw their pistols. Randy shot one barrel between two men and the other barrel between the remaining two men. All four men went down as several of their pistols fired at the floor during the gunplay. Randy checked the outlaws and found three were dead. The other was barely alive as Randy asks, "why did you draw on me, I had you covered with a shotgun?"

"Well deputy, we're all wanted men, dead or alive, with money on our heads. We had no choice," as he took his last breath.

Minutes later, Sheriff Wilcox steps in the saloon. "I was on my way to the privy when I head all the shooting. What happened here Scotty?

Scotty the bartender says, "one of the dead men shot an unarmed man. When confronted by Deputy McWain, he and his three boys drew and tried to shoot your deputy. Deputy McWain stood his ground and put all four down with two shots of his sawed-off shotgun. Your deputy has sand and it was a good shoot. You chose well with this young man."

That night, Randy didn't sleep much. By predawn, he had the coffee brewing as he was going thru reward posters. He found the four posters that matched the dead men. All four were wanted for murder, rape, and robbery. Dead or Alive with a reward of $500 each.

When the sheriff arrived, he said, "after the shooting, every patron in that bar agreed with Scotty. You were lucky, and I'm so glad you had your shotgun. Now let's go thru wanted posters."

"Here they are!"

Sam goes over the posters and says, "I'm going to the telegraph to notify the ones posting the rewards. You will be due $2,000 on your first day at work, heh!"

The weeks to follow were a low-key affair. Sheriff Wilcox accompanied Randy on rounds morning and afternoon. Randy did the evening rounds by himself. During the days, Sam went over several scenarios and how to handle each one safely. These included discussions on saloon arrests, marital discord and abuse, tracking tips, serving processes, threats of bodily harm, ambush, merchant robberies, setting up a safe trail camp, and the two methods of running down killer/robber gangs—the posse method vs. individual lawman.

With Sam's experience and instructions, Randy felt he was ready to deal with the demands of the job. One day during evening rounds, Randy went to check-out the weekly dog fight at the railroad yard. As much as he despised the event, it was allowed by the town council since it brought business into town—and of course the council members were all town merchants.

There was a total of six fights. The first five were limited events where a dog owner could stop a fight if his losing dog was getting beaten. Other than taking a loss, this would allow the dog to fight again. The last fight was a fight to the end. Randy watched the first five events and agreed with the process. The last event was brutal. A large mastiff was overpowering a large mutt. The mutt collapsed and the mastiff's owner called his dog off. The mutt, a cross between a collie and a German Sheppard. looked dead and was dragged off the ring.

After the crowd paid off their bets and

cleared the area, the mutt's owner was standing over the animal and was about to shoot him. Randy hollered, "whoa there, is that dog alive?"

"Barely, I'm going to put him out of his misery."

"Wait, I'll give you $5 for the animal."

"It's a waste of your money, but I'll take it."

As Randy was checking out the dog, a man came up and offered the use of his buckboard to bring the animal to his office. Once at the office, Randy was reassured that the injuries included many deep bites and a lot of blood loss. Randy offered the dog water on a plate and the dog lapped several platefuls. An antiseptic salve was rubbed over the deep bites and a blanket was used to keep the animal warm next to the coal stove. Several times during the night, Randy got up to offer the dog more water and the last time he fed him some left over beef stew. By morning, Randy was awakened by some strange feeling on his hand—the dog was standing over Randy and licking his hand.

"Well, it looks like you are going to make it, heh! I bet you want some breakfast?" The dog looked at Randy and cocked his head sideways in a questioning position. Randy warmed up the remainder of the beef stew which was quickly inhaled by the hungry beast.

Afterwards Randy said, "well for a dog who was barely alive, you look pretty solid to me. I guess you are as solid as a rock, so I'll call you Rocky from now on"—as the dog cocked his head sideways again.

When Sam arrived at 8AM, he was surprised and pleased to see a huge mutt next to Randy. He quickly realized that this would be a beneficial adage to Randy's security. He cautiously stepped over to the dog and patted his head until the long tail started to wag. Sam added, "this animal looks intelligent but will need a lot of training to make him your partner on the trail. I'll be happy to help you train him."

Every afternoon, when things were quiet, Sam would man the fort and allow Randy to go to the range to practice shooting and train Rocky. His practice sessions were spent on the sawed-off shotgun and the long- range Win 76 rifle, since he was already proficient with fast draw, pistol shooting, and free-style rifle shooting to 100 yards.

The shotgun had been modified from a long shoulder stock to a short pistol grip. He practiced drawing the shotgun by grabbing the pistol grip and pulling it out of the holster. He learned how to cock both mule ears back with his left hand while holding the pistol grip with his right hand. Now placing his left hand under the forearm and keeping the shotgun at waist level, he was able to fire the shotgun. In this position, he practiced shooting it till he was able to hit a 16-inch board at 7 and 18 yards and hitting it repeatedly by point and shoot without aiming.

His Win 76 had a 8X Malcolm scope. Shooting it at 200 yards was a cinch, but 300-400 was new to him. It took a long time shooting off a rest to come close to a man size target at those distances. Once Randy managed how to set the elevation scope settings for the different yardage, he started to get on target. It was a new way of shooting that had to be learned.

His practice sessions always included some

fast draw and pistol shooting as well as free style 100-yard rifle shooting. During the shooting, Rocky patiently waited since he knew his training would follow the shooting.

Rocky was a willing and quick learner. Randy taught him to track by the scent, how to attack on command, how to kill on command, how to recognize a friend, how to warn and defend a trail camp, how to warn him of impending danger from another man, how to warn him of an oncoming ambush, and how to warn him of camp smoke. Beyond this, Rocky was generally protective of Randy, his horse and his friends. In public, Rocky behaved like a mild mannered and well-behaved massive dog. Randy knew that he would become an essential asset whether in town or on the trail.

The six month's training came to an end and Sheriff Wilcox was confident that Randy was ready for independent service. A few weeks later while on afternoon rounds, Randy was accosted by a gunfighter waiting in front of the Wet Bucket Saloon.

"Stop right there, deputy, I am calling you out and I'm going to kill you and your dog."

"Who are you and why me?"

"My name is Deuce Muldoon and months ago, you killed my brother and his gang in Wilder's Saloon. Now this is my revenge, so go for your gun or I will."

Rocky could sense danger and started growling. Randy added, "sit Rocky, and sir if you go for your gun, I will have to shoot you. Now by the looks of your rig, I may not be as fast as you but I'm very accurate. I will end up shooting you in the chest even if you hit me first. Now is it really your time to die, or is it time to ride out of town?"

Without any hesitation, Muldoon went for his gun and lifted it out of the holster as a shot ran out. Muldoon was pushed back with a look of surprise on his face, as he crumbled to the ground. People were talking and came to congratulate Randy for defending himself. Sheriff Wilcox arrived on the scene and recognized Muldoon from reward posters. He looked at Randy and asked, "was this a good shoot?" Before he could answer, the crowd erupted. Everyone was trying to speak in Randy's defense. Pure self-defense was the consensus.

Sheriff Wilcox was heard saying, "word of this gunfight will spread all over Texas. Every yahoo trying to make a reputation for himself will want to have a try against Randy—only to their demise."

Out of Randy's control, a telegraph voucher arrived in the sum of $750 for Muldoon's capture. Randy went to the town bank, where his dad worked, and opened an account with the now total sum of $2,750 from Muldoon's gang and brother. Little did he know this account would grow under a mix of circumstances.

***

CHAPTER 4

RANDY'S CHANGE OF PROFESSION

For days after the shootout, Randy had been soul searching. It was a revelation to get $2,750 for doing his job. It seemed to him that being a deputy sheriff would only rarely bring such an opportunity again. Besides, what is he to do with so much money. It was Sam who came to a reluctant answer.

"Randy, you can do so much good to help the poor families in this settlement. The homesteaders are all lacking the basics, food and clothing. To give you an idea, go to Harper's Mercantile and buy two dime novels— biographies of Wayne Swanson and Cal

Harnell. Both were well known paladin bounty hunters who amassed large amounts of money and developed a method of distributing their fortune. I am reluctant to make this suggestion since it smells like I'm trying to get rid of you. Far from the truth, but a necessary exposure to your future."

For days Randy read the evenings away under a coal lamp. He learned new techniques in handling the deadly killers and found out how their benefactor funds were doing so much good. Beyond these two benefits, he found out what it meant to be a Paladin—a person dedicated to ridding the world of evil and destructive outlaws. Following the book recommendations, Randy purchased manacles, chains, padlocks, an awl and marlin nail, and had a blacksmith build some steel neck collars. He also purchased an extra horse. He needed to have a packhorse with paniers and a saddle for his dog, just like Cal Harnell had for his dog.

The paniers were filled with the usual trail necessities. A change of clothes, tarp, cooking grill, frying pan, cooking pot, coffee pot, rain slicker, utensils, sewing kit, carbolic acid, razor/ kit and tooth powder/brush. Other preparation items included one pommel holster, two large saddle bags and a total of four scabbards—to fit the Win 73, Win 76 with scope, long standard shotgun and the sawed-off shotgun.

By the time he read both books, he had accumulated his trail gear, and everything sat in the livery's storage room along with a list of food items for Schilling's Mercantile. While reading the two biographical novels, Randy had marked special pages that he wanted to reread and even carefully study. And so, at the present time, Randy was in limbo. Should he continue his current position as a deputy or resign and hit the dangerous trail as a bounty hunter? Two things happened that helped him reach a decision.

Sheriff Wilcox received a telegram from a nearby town's elderly sheriff. Sheriff Moe Sims from Tupperville. Apparently, a brutal miscreant, Isadore Lord, owned a whore house and was keeping his local girls locked up and forced to work against their will. The elderly sheriff was requesting assistance to arrest the owner and his three men. and close down the whorehouse.

The other bit of information was that these local girls had been kidnapped by Lord's men from outlying ranches. Every rancher had filed kidnapping charges against Lord, and so Sheriff Simms had to arrest and charge the man with kidnapping and imprisoning people.

Sam and Randy discussed the situation and decided that Randy would be the more capable lawman to handle these four men. So, Randy packed his saddlebags and headed out the next morning with Rocky. By mid afternoon they arrived in Tupperville and took a room in a hotel. After an early dinner, Randy went to see Sheriff Sims.

Randy walks in the sheriff's office and Sheriff Sims says, "what can I do for you son?"

"My name is Deputy Sheriff Randy McWain and Sheriff Wilcox has sent me to help you with the Lord problem."

"Where are the other deputies?"

"I'm alone, now tell me a bit more about the layout and where the men can be found."

"Well Ok, but it's your funeral. I will bring you to Lord's place but I'm not going in with you. I'm too old for such antics. So, I'll stay outside with a wagon to receive the bodies."

When they arrived at Lord's place of business, Randy entered with Rocky at his side. He was immediately greeted by Isadore himself who yells, "dogs are not allowed in here, get that cur out of here, now."

Randy responds, "that's not going to happen."

"Suit yourself, boys, throw this bum out."

"Stop, I'm a deputy sheriff, as he opens his vest to show his badge on his shirt. You are all under arrest."

As two men step up and grab Randy's arms, Randy immediately realized that decisive action needed to take place with these two bouncers. After a few steps towards the door, Randy released his right arm, pulled out his backpack shotgun and smacks the man on his right across the head with the shotgun's barrel. At the next moment, the man on his left let go of Randy's arm and went for his gun. The shotgun's barrel made immediate contact with this second man and both were found laid out on the floor.

As Randy turned to face Lord, another man had his gun drawn as Randy shot him point blank in mid chest as blood splattered over Lord's face. Isadore was shocked to see his three men down and became instantly furious. "I'm going to kill you with my bare hands."

As Isadore stepped up and grabbed Randy by the shirt, Randy decided to perform a trick that he had practiced many times. Randy stood firm, pulled the hammer back on his holstered Colt, angle the holster forward and a bit to the left and pulled the trigger. The bullet left the bottom of the open toe holster and smacked directly in Isadore's boot top. Isadore quickly collapsed to the floor screaming and holding his perforated boot with blood flowing out of both holes.

"Well Rocky, I finally got to try this well practiced trick, heh," as the dog cocked his head sideways.

Over the next two days, the girls were

reunited with their husbands and families, Isadore had received medical attention and all three men were scheduled for a trial once the circuit judge arrived. To Randy's surprise, Lord and his gang all had old warrants for their arrests for kidnapping and Randy received a bonus $1500 in telegraph vouchers which he pocketed for a later deposit in his hometown bank.

Arriving back home, Randy was sent to serve some divorce papers. to one mean rancher by the name of Vance Stapleton. Marguerite Stapleton had been brought to Doc Tibbs for care. She had switch marks over her body, a busted jaw and nose with blown out orbits and trapped eye movements. Plus, she had been in a deep coma for three weeks. Now, following legal advice, she was applying for a divorce and financial compensation to the tune of $15,000—which was half the estimated value of the ranch house, land and cattle. As an addendum, for a quick non contested divorce, the claimant would accept a final payment of $11,000.

Randy never hesitated, he rode to the

Stapleton ranch with Rocky and stepped on the porch. With a loud knock, he heard a gruff voice saying, "stop pounding on the door, I'm coming."

As the door opened, Randy said, "per court order, I am serving you with these divorce papers."

Stapleton grabbed the papers, read the order to appear in divorce court and immediately got to fuming. "It's been three weeks and so I assumed the bitch was dead, so she appears to be alive. Tell the lawyer that she's not getting a penny."

"No sir, that's not how it works. You have to appear in court and speak for yourself. I suggest you get your own lawyer."

"Better still, show your battered face to the bitch's lawyer and tell him that's what his face will look like if he doesn't drop these proceedings." As Stapleton pulls his right arm back, Rocky takes a bite out of his calf, as Randy watches Stapleton hop around screaming like a rabbit in a trap.

Once Rocky was called off, Stapleton was

moaning about the obvious teeth marks in his calf. "If you weren't hiding behind a cur dog, I'd show you what I would do to that lawyer and judge."

"Be glad to." Randy removes his badge and drops his gunbelt to the porch floor, steps inside and closes the door with Rocky left on the porch.

Stapleton came after Randy with a smile on his face. The smile changed to a grimace as Randy applied a clipping side kick to Stapleton's left knee. Popping ligaments were clearly heard as Stapleton fell to the floor with his left lower leg at a strange unnatural angle. Randy then said, "now I'm going to give you what you gave to your wife."

Randy spotted a hard wood switch by the door. He grabbed it and hit Stapleton over every sensitive part of his body. Then he punched him in the face till he broke his jaw, blew out one orbit, and turned his face to a crushed tomato.

At the end of the beating, Randy said, "you were lucky, I didn't put you into a three-week coma. But, if you contest this divorce, I will be back and gladly place you in this coma. Needless to say, this meeting never took place if you know what is good for you."

On his way back to town, Randy found himself woolgathering. It was clear that this man needed to be punished for abusing his wife. Had he done this to any other person, he would end up in prison for attempted murder. Hiding behind the rights of husbands over their wives, was a perceived law handed down over the years. It was clear that the law had no control over this problem. Did removing his gun and badge protect the lawman in providing justice. Well, it was clear to Randy if this is what Sam wanted, then he had made the right decision to send him to do the deed and not try to do this himself at his age.

As he entered town from the east, a gunshot was heard at the other end of town. Randy went down Main street at a full gallop as he passed Sam running down the boardwalk with shotgun in hand. As Randy arrived at the bank, the outlaws were mounting their horses and shooting at Randy and innocent bystanders.

Randy quickly pulled out his sawed-off shotgun, pulled back both hammers, aimed high to not hit the horses. and let off both barrels. To his surprise two outlaws fell out of the saddle, one of which was holding a money bag. The other three robbers got away at full gallop.

After the shooting stopped, the head teller came out and confirmed that the money bag had the contents of US currency from the vault. The money bag that got away only had petty cash from the cashiers to a maximum of $200. The saved vault currency came to $3,000. Randy was getting ready to go after the remaining three outlaws when the head teller stopped him. "Randy, your dad was in charge of the bank with the bank president at a council meeting. When the gang leader brought your dad in the vault, he ordered your dad to fill his bag. Your dad opened the first drawer where a pistol was hidden. He grabbed the gun, but the outlaw saw the gun coming out of the drawer and shot your dad down. He's in very bad shape. You need to go to him, now."

Randy rushed into the bank and found his

dad in the vault. His dad spoke, "It's better this way son, I had to try to save the bank's solvency. Besides, a quick death is better than being eaten alive by cancer of the bone marrow. When I'm gone talk to Doc Tibbs for an explanation and inform your mother. Promise me only one thing, when I'm gone take care of the most important woman in my entire life, your mother." As he took his last breaths on this earth.

Seeing how distraught Randy was, Sheriff Wilcox started organizing a posse to go after the killer gang. Randy stopped the sheriff and said, "there is no reason to put our people in danger, this is my job and I'll bring these murderers back, dead or alive."

Within a half hour, his two horses were saddled. The packhorse had the prepacked paniers attached and also loaded with trail food for him and Rocky. Randy realized, as he left the town limits, this was his first hunt of killer outlaws and also his last job for his hometown.

***

With four hours of daylight remaining, Randy kept his horses and Rocky at a slow trot. After two hours on the trail, Randy stopped at a stream to water the horses. Rocky was "done in" and did not need much encouragement to hop on the packhorse platform above the paniers, for the next two hours before dark. At dark, Randy found an ideal camp location with a fresh spring and plenty of new grass. He presumed that the outlaws would keep riding under moonlight for the first night after a job. Randy could not take the chance of following at night for fear of walking into a fatal ambush. He figured that the outlaws would stop some time tomorrow and if he was lucky, would catch up with them before dark.

That night, Randy made a decent cooking fire and cooked fried potatoes, onions, and three beef steaks along with a full pot of coffee. One steak was cooked to a pink center but the other two were raw for Rocky. Of course, Rocky got all three bones. After dinner and cleaning utensils, Randy got a good night's sleep with his pistol on his right side of his bedroll and Rocky and his sawed-off shotgun on the other side. In the morning, Randy had coffee, beans and bacon while Rocky had his favorite oatmeal porridge flavored with sorghum and any leftovers. This concoction was the only affordable food for dogs in an area of the world where food came at a premium.

By daybreak, Randy had, cleaned and closed camp, and was on the road. It was a long eight hours of tracking and riding when Rocky started sniffing the air. It was clear that Rocky was smelling campfire smoke. The horses were ground hitched and Randy followed Rocky on foot till he could see their camp some 300 yards away. Using his 50X binoculars, he was able to spy on the camp. The outlaws were drinking heavily and would soon be half gone. So, Randy waited till two of the men were asleep. The gang leader was awake and clearly upset at the small take of cash from the last job. With two sleeping and one clearly preoccupied, Randy decided to make an appearance.

Quietly, Randy sneaked up on the camp with his sawed-off shotgun in his hands. Within 20 yards, he speaks out. "You're all under arrest for bank robbery and murder of a bank clerk. Put your hands up. The leader said, "you're the deputy who killed two of my men and took back the vault money."

"Yes, and you're the man who shot the bank teller. That was my father and he died."

All three outlaws knew they were facing an angry lawman who wanted retribution, and all three went for their guns simultaneously.

Randy saw the event happening in slow motion. The gang leader had his two men to his right and was drawing his pistol from his right hand. When the guns came out of their holsters, Randy squeezed both triggers and the two men dropped from the shotgun blasts. To Randy's surprise, the pistol from the leader fell to the ground. It was clear, after the fact, that a #3 Buckshot had hit the gang leader in the arm causing the pistol to fall out of his hand.

Randy slowly walked to the gang leader and said, "for killing my father, I'm going to beat you to a pulp and your face is going to look like you were kicked in the face by an angry horse." Without any warning, Randy started pummeling his face, the nose got flattened, teeth went flying, pieces of his lips were dangling, and his eyes were turning purple. The jaw was broken twice, and one earlobe was pulverized to meatloaf.

The outlaw collapsed and Randy placed the manacles on him as well as a neck collar with a chain padlocked to a tree. Randy then checked each outlaw's pockets and was able to collect $729 which he pocketed. He collected three new Colts, three new Win 73, three saddled horses which he would eventually sell. Finally, he set up camp for the night and planned to bring all three outlaws to his hometown.

After two days on the trail, Randy finally arrived home. He went straight to the sheriff's office and deposited his catch. Sheriff Wilcox took one look at the survivor and said, "the one hit by a train looks a lot worse than the two dead ones."

"That's because there was no train in the vicinity, so I used a 10- pound sledgehammer, heh!"

The next day, Sheriff Wilcox was able to identify the entire gang with names. Checking with the telegraph, he found that they were all wanted men, dead or alive. He arranged for vouchers to be sent to pay Randy. The total for all five men was $1,500. A few days later when he went to the bank to deposit these vouchers, he gave the bank $229 to replace the estimated stolen money from the cashiers. The $1,500 was then deposited into his mother's account as well as the $1000 in life insurance the bank was owing to Randy's mother.

Afterwards, he had a long visit with his mother. After getting past the emotions, he explained to her how Doc Tibbs had found a bone marrow cancer that would be a painful terminal disease. Randy explained that she had over three thousand dollars in the bank and when she needed more, he would provide her financial needs. The last bit of bad news, Randy explained that he was leaving town for an unknown period. He explained his need to rid the world of evil men in order for peaceful men to thrive. This would be a temporary service to his fellow man, but for now was his only goal in life.

The next day, Randy met with Sheriff Wilcox. Sam knew what was coming but still listened intently to Randy's reason for leaving his job and becoming a bounty hunter. Randy offered to stay two weeks to allow Sam to train a new recruit. Sam chose against it. Sam admitted that he enjoyed training Randy and had another candidate in mind.

Randy stayed in town for the trial. During the trial, he kept looking at his father's murderer. He regretted beating this man. It was too dehumanizing. The more he watched the man barely holding his head up, the outlaw seemed to perk up when the verdict was read as guilty and he was sentenced to hang. At least his agony would soon come to an end.

It was this trial revelation that convinced Randy to bring his outlaws back either dead or alive, but not beaten or tortured. If an outlaw gave up, he would be brought back alive and unscathed. If an outlaw drew a gun on him, he would be shot dead or wounded. If information was needed from an outlaw, he would not physically torture the man but would use the awl method established by Swanson and Harnell.

***

CHAPTER 5

THE SOLO YEAR

Before his departure, Randy had a few errands to run. He went to the local apothecary and bought two bottles of different scents. One was cedar and the other was pine scent. Being in semi deserts and plains will allow the scent to hold on the ground. His next stop was the blacksmith shop. He had ordered two more neck collars with lightweight chains, manacles and padlocks.

At Schilling's Mercantile, to get some beef jerky for himself and Rocky, he learned of a new item. Dried vegetable and beef dog food by the bag. He took a sample and offered it to Rocky, who just about inhaled it in two gulps.

His last stop was the sheriff's office. As Randy walked in, he said, "I'm here to return my badge."

"Keep it, you may need it on some capers and if I get a question about its validity, I'll confirm the fact that you are on special assignment. Now, by the time you ever come back home, the railroad is in the process of choosing a major depot between Amarillo and Wichita Falls. That is a 200 mile stretch and our hometown is halfway to each town. There is talk of combining our town and the neighboring community and call it Childress. The railroad will build a depot to include coal reserves, a ticket office, a new hotel, several stock yards with loading ramps and side rails with a turn table. The office will have its own vault to hold cash for the incoming cattle. This means growth over a short time and it may mean that I may need your help to control gangs. So, keep in touch thru the local lawmen so I can find you if necessary."

"Will do, and never hesitate to contact me.

I will always be within reach of the railroad between Amarillo and Wichita Falls. For now, I'm taking the train to Wichita Falls and start my 200-mile northwest trac to Amarillo."

Arriving in Wichita Falls, Randy brought his two horses and Rocky to the nearest livery. Left some beef jerky and dry dog food for Rocky and headed to the nearest hotel with his guns and saddlebags. After a full lunch at the hotel restaurant, Randy went to find the local lawman and found two—a county sheriff and a city marshal. The city marshal was Marshal Omer McDonald, an elderly well-seasoned lawman with one deputy. After introductions were done, Randy started.

"I'm a bounty hunter looking for outlaws who may be in your town. Can I look at your wanted posters"

"Sure, but for the past six months, things have been quiet in town. It seems that all criminal activity is located in the next town, Mineville."

"Why is that and tell me more."

"Mineville is a small settlement 20 miles

west of here. It basically serves the 'Smith Gold Mine' a mile north of the town. In the past, payroll was done at the bank in town, but that failed when many of the workers were waylaid on their way back to the mine where they live and work. The loss of life and workers put an end to this payment method. Recently they tried to send the payroll with the ore cars being side tracked to the mine. That also failed when the outlaws blew the tracks with dynamite, derailed the ore cars, and stole the payroll. Several payrolls have been stolen and the insurance company is threatening to cancel the mine's policy."

"I hear the current method is a bullet proof stagecoach built to transport workers, mine executives and the payroll cash box to the mine. The problem is that they can't find anyone to drive or protect the stagecoach. They need a jehu and a shotgun guard. At the moment, the county sheriff, George Samuels is in Mineville trying to organize the first coach to the mine. If you're looking for work, I'd head out there. The pay is $200 per ride to the mine and back, but if you arrest or kill outlaws that have a bounty on their heads, the bounty is yours as is their guns, personal belongings and horses."

"I'll take it, when is the next train to Mineville, and would you send a telegram to Sheriff Samuels?"

"Head for the depot, the train leaves in one hour and I'll inform George of your arrival today."

Thanks to some flat terrain, the train made the 20-mile trip to Mineville in a half hour, depot to depot. To achieve this, the train maintained 40 mph—certainly better than sitting in the saddle for four plus hours.

On the Mineville platform stood a lawman waiting for passengers. Randy went to him and they walked away as Sheriff Samuels started to explain the specifics of the job.

"This, as explained to you by the city marshal, is the third attempt to get men and money safely from Mineville to the Smith Mine. The two passengers are the mine owner and a major investor from Chicago. The payroll for twelve days is roughly $8,000 to cover some

200 men—or each man makes roughly $3 a day for a 10-hour day."

"Marshal McDonald said, this was a bullet proof coach. What does that mean?"

"The jehu's footwell has a steel plate added in front of his knees. In case of a frontal attack, he can drop down in the footwell for some protection. The back of the driver's seat also has a plate of steel to protect the passengers from a frontal attack. The rear of the coach has a steel plate to again protect the passengers from a rearward attack. The coach walls are not protected."

"The stagecoach makes the run once a day to transport sick or injured workers or other important personnel. The payroll cash box is included on every trip. Randomly, one trip every two weeks, the cash box has the payroll—and that day is not publicized."

"And of course, with internal spies, we fear the outlaws may know which coach to attack."

"I suspect you're right. So, tomorrow the cash box is hot. I'll be the jehu, you'll be the shotgun guard, we are carrying two executives and $8,000 in US currency.

"That's about it, so see you in the morning."

The next morning, Randy arrived with his full length and his sawed-off shotgun. Picked up the coach shotgun out of the driver's foot-well and said to Sheriff Samuels, "if you are confronted with outlaws in your face, drop to the footwell floor-board and drive the team thru them. I will be in the boot to greet them. If they come from behind, get down and keep driving. I'll be back there to surprise them as I lift the tarp off the boot and start shooting."

"Unconventional, but I like your plan. Will do."

"As they were making ready, the two passengers were warned that the side of the coach was not bullet proof. If outlaws made it past the shotgun guard, they were expected to shoot at them thru the windows with their own shotguns."

The ride was fairly smooth since the coach was following the rail bed used by the ore cars. Without warning, a large group of outlaws started chasing the stagecoach. Randy saw them from his hideout behind the boot tarp. As they were almost up to the coach, they started shooting at Sheriff Samuels. That is when Randy lifted the tarp, threw it behind him, and pulled up his sawed-off shotgun. With two blast, the nearest outlaws were blown out of the saddle. Quickly, picking up the other two shotguns, another four riders were knocked off their horses. The two remaining outlaws pulled to the side and disappeared from view.

Realizing the robbery had been thwarted, Sheriff Samuels stopped the coach to check on Randy and the two passengers. All were well and the Chicago investor was very appreciative of Randy's performance and said, "young man, I appreciate your fine gun work and I owe you. So, if you ever need a favor, feel free to call on me. My name is Winston Montgomery Ward."

Randy went to check on all the outlaws. The pockets were emptied and came up to $489 in coin and paper currency. The gunbelts and pistols were stored in the saddle bags and the outlaws were straddled over the saddle with feet and hands tied together to secure them on the horse. Trailing the stagecoach on a rope, the six outlaw horses with their cargo continued their trek to the mine without further incidents.

After getting back to Mineville, Sheriff Samuels had checked and found the six dead outlaws were wanted by the law for murder and robbery. The total rewards came to $3,000 which would be paid by telegraph vouchers once Randy returned to Mineville.

Over the next week, Randy agreed to stay on the job as shotgun guard. The pay was good at $200 per trip but Randy also felt other gangs of outlaws would take over, especially the two outlaws who escaped from the first robbery. What no one realized was that Randy was trying to get to the source of spying by identifying the traitor.

Randy went to the local bank, the Mineville First National. He had a long talk with President Wakefield. All the working clerks were married men with years of dedicated service, except for one. This young man was Steve Golden, son of the town mayor. President Wakefield agreed to release a special shipment of extra cash to the mine. Randy followed the single clerk after work and saw him enter a local saloon. Following the clerk inside, he saw him talking to another patron standing at the bar. When the clerk left, Randy followed the unidentified patron to his horse.

Rushing to the livery, Randy saddled his horse and took off to follow the presumed outlaw to his camp. One hour later, he saw the smoke from the camp fire and could even hear the gang talk about the news of the current cash shipment. The gang had again grown to eight members and Randy knew that he needed to get some help to round up this small army.

What really impressed Randy was the discussion of how they planned to take over the stagecoach. The gang's leader said, "We're going to place our men with rifles along the road. I'm going to shoot one of the four horses pulling the stagecoach—which guarantees the stagecoach will stop on the spot. You men will shoot, using your rifles, from a hidden location. Everyone dies, we leave no witnesses."

At that point, Randy retreated to organize and fight another day. Arriving in town, he filled in Sheriff Samuels. A frontal attack on eight gunfighters would be suicide for the two of them. They needed an advantage, such as some impaired outlaws, if they were to capture this gang. That is when Randy thought of the two dime novels he had been reading. The answer was guerilla warfare.

The cash shipment would be in seven days, so Randy knew he had time to set this guerilla attack in time. There would be no way this gang would not run out of whiskey, and the nearest supply was at the mercantile in Mineville. Randy had bought eight bottles of whiskey and placed them in a crate. He added two potent large animal remedies to each bottle and returned them to the mercantile. The owner, Claude Gray, agreed to hold this crate for the outlaws that Randy would identify ahead of time.

Randy and Rocky had been hiding out along the trail leading out of the outlaw camp. On the third morning, a rider leading a packhorse came by. Randy left the trail and rode hard cross country to get to Gray's Mercantile before the outlaw got there.

The outlaw loaded with supplies and eight bottles of "hot" whiskey and headed back to camp. Sheriff Samuels, Rocky and Randy took off for the outlaw camp some four hours later. Arriving some 200 yards from camp, Rocky went wild from the odor of fresh human feces that everyone could smell. Above the smell was the roar of men vomiting.

As Randy and Sheriff Samuels arrived to within eye's view of the carnage, a sight was hard to believe. Every outlaw was either pooping on the spot or retching at the same time. No one had any energy to go into the bushes to privately take care of their urges.

"Well Randy, your guerilla warfare certainly worked. Maybe I should read the same dime novels as you did. Meanwhile, how do we gather these animals without getting our clothing or hands dirty?"

"We wait till the retching and pooping stops, then throw them in the river with their clothing and a bar of soap. Then we manacle them to the saddle and bring them to jail to stand trial—I'm certain they all are wanted dead or alive. They will all be dehydrated from the 'cleansing' and won't be much of a threat to ride them back to town."

As Randy had suspected, they were all wanted criminals. The total rewards came to $4,000 which Randy gave half to Sheriff Samuels. The criminals were transferred by prison wagon back to Wichita Falls where the trial was held. Three were hung and five were given prison sentences, including the bank spy.

After the trial, Randy spent a week enjoying the sights of a small well-organized city. He had a nice hotel room with a water closet and bath. He had several diners for his meals and even played some friendly games of poker. Randy liked an occasional cold beer if kept on ice.

Since Whichita Falls had an ice house insulated with sawdust, cold beer was available in most saloons until the ice ran out. The week of leisure came to an end when Marshal McDonald showed up one morning at Sally's diner and joined Randy at his table.

"Well Randy, you did a fine job to clean up the thieves in Mineville. Are you available for another caper that smells to high heaven?"

"Might be, what do you have in mind."

"Human extortion, kidnapping and rape from psychopaths."

"You have my attention, tell me more."

"In a small town west of here, called Brunson Station, there is a gang of men who have taken over a town. They drink in all the saloons, eat in three diners, pick up items from the merchants, use services such as bath houses and laundry services, reside in the local hotel and of late have commandeered a house for sale and made it their own whore house. Are you getting the drift, yet"

"I hear you, but I must be missing something."

"Well they are living off the town and have paid nothing. Any merchant who confronts them for money gets beaten to the ground. The last insult, they have kidnapped some local gals to service themselves.

They are kept under lock and key. One of the husbands showed up with a shogun to free his wife. The poor soul has been in a coma for ten days and is not expected to survive. In another instance, Butch's Diner refused to serve this gang. He has gone missing now for two weeks and his wife is selling the diner so she can leave town."

"I see, and what is expected of me?"

"The town council wants you to get the gang to pay back the cost of their expenditures and free the imprisoned ladies. If any have wanted posters on them, you can dispose of them as you see fit and keep the rewards and their belongings."

"So, the pay is the bounty on their heads, if it exists."

"Yes, plus 10% of any secured back payment. The council will also name you a temporary sheriff with a badge. Just keep in mind, the original town sheriff was found drowned in a nearby river the same week this gang arrived."

"I just can't believe how some evil men can be so dehumanizing without a care for their fellow man. I will take the job because of the captive women and the need for financial restitution.

Once I've rescued the women, I'll take care of these men."

***

Arriving in town by train, Randy was met by the town mayor—Mayor Stan Brunson. "Good day Mr. McWain and thank you for taking this job. We certainly need your help and you come highly recommended by Sheriff McDonald."

They then walked to the sheriff's office. Randy was sworn in and given his badge. He was shown where to put his guns, his private bedroom in the back, given the combination to the safe, given a set of keys to the cells and the office front and back door.

After the mayor left, he brought his horse to the town livery. He asked what the back pay was for this troublesome gang. The hostler said, "eight horses for three weeks at 75 cents a day comes to $126. Randy says, "I'll be back to settle with you after I get your money"

Randy realized that the imprisoned women were first to be dealt with. Randy got directions from the livery man and went straight to the gang's house with Rocky at his side. Stepping on the porch, he knocked and waited for the door to open. A scruffy man holding his head from an apparent hangover rudely said, "who do you think you are coming to this restricted house. I'm going to pistol whip you."

As the bum put his hand on his pistol grip, Randy stepped into his face, pounded his boot heel onto the man's toes and stepped on his foot.

The man screamed out as Randy relieved him of his pistol, slammed the pistol's hammer against the door jam, and bent the hammer out of function. Randy then asked, "who is the leader of your gang and how many men are in the house right now?"

When the outlaw refused to answer, Randy pulled his pistol and firmly tapped the man's front teeth. Both teeth broke off at the gum line. The man was so taken by surprise that he quickly blurted out, "one man in the kitchen and the boss is Clem Crutchfield."

Randy sent Rocky into the kitchen as he placed the manacles on his man. The dog's roar came to life as he heard the outlaw beg for his life. By the time Randy stepped in the kitchen there was fresh blood all over the floor. When Rocky was called off, the outlaw was more than agreeable to accept the manacles. The upstairs bedroom door was then unlocked, and the two gals were rescued.

Getting to the office with two ladies and two outlaws, as they opened the office door, Mayor Brunson was sitting at the desk with a double barrel coach shotgun on the desk. "What are you doing here, Stan.

"I figured you needed someone to guard the prisoners and protect these two ladies. Let me introduce you to Myra Steele and Cindy Lane. While you are out dealing with the remainder of the gang, I'll make sure these ladies are not harmed, and your prisoners don't escape."

Randy emptied the outlaw's pockets of cash and placed $97 in his own pocket. Then his first errand was to send a telegram to Sheriff McDonald inquiring if Clem Crutchfield and his gang had any bounty on their heads. Then he went looking for gang members. His first stop was the "Beer Barrel Saloon." Stepping thru the batwing doors, the bartender was about to object to a dog in his saloon but hesitated when he saw Randy's badge. Randy asked for a beer and wanted to know if any of the gang was in the saloon. The bartender pointed to two men sitting at their own table with an empty whiskey bottle between them.

Randy quietly stepped to the table and slammed his hunting knife thru the top of one man's hand. The impaled outlaw's scream and facial look of pain quickly sobered his partner who went for his gun. Rocky grabbed his gun hand and now both men were screaming like wild hyenas.

Without releasing the men, he asks the bartender how much these men owed him. Two bottles of whiskey each day at $4 each for the past three weeks comes to roughly $88. Randy empties the outlaw's pockets and takes $100 out for the bartender. The balance of $201 went into Randy's pockets.

When he got back to the office with two more prisoners, the telegrapher was waiting for him. The telegram from Sheriff McDonald guaranteed that Clem Crutchfield had a $1000 reward, wanted dead or alive, for murder and bank robbery. The other seven men were also wanted dead or alive, for a multitude of crimes, and their bounty totaled $3500.

Now the jail cells were full but could be doubled up if the last four men were captured alive. Randy doubted that would happen. Crutchfield would likely know that their women were gone, that they were short of four men, and would be coming for the culprit.

Clem Crutchfield and his three toadies had just been at the local bank to negotiate a protection contract with the bank president, Stuart Bellows. For a fee of $25 a week, Clem would provide security against robberies. When he got to the house, his guards and whores were gone. Furious beyond belief, he sent two men south of town as he and his second in command went north of town looking for his missing men and women.

Randy was sitting on the boardwalk next to his office when two well healed men came towards him. Randy stood and ordered them to stop. He asks, "are you with Clem Crutchfield?"

"Yes, and where did you come from?"

"From Wichita Falls, sent here to pick you pieces of crap up and get you to pay your debts. Besides, I hear you have a bounty on your heads, dead or alive."

"Get out of our way or say your prayers, sonny."

"No, you're under arrest. Put your hands up."

Their hands moved, but not to point upwards, they both went for their guns. Randy responded with a quick draw and shot one man and fanned a second shot to the other man. Both went down and were dead before they hit the boardwalk.

As shots were heard, Clem and his man quickly did an about face and raced to check on his men. When they got to the sheriff's office, the new sheriff was seen checking the outlaw's pockets. Clem yells out, "hey you, get away from those men. Who are you anyway?"

"I'm the temporary law in town and your extortion and abuse days are over. Raise your hands, your both under arrest. You can't beat my draw and if you try, you'll both die."

"We're both wanted dead or alive, and you are not arresting us to die at the end of a rope."

Seeing both men draw, Randy plugged Clem's partner in the head but shot the pistol out of Clem's hand. Stepping up to Clem he said, "wrong, you are going to hang."

A few days later, Randy added up all the cash he had collected from the outlaws and it came to $688. Totaling all the unpaid debts incurred by this gang, he came to a final amount of $2246. That meant that Clem had a hiding place somewhere and Randy was determined to find it. Clem had to have a cache from years of robbing banks.

Randy went to the jail and pulled Clem to the back office. Securing him to the bed frame, he straddled him and opened his mouth. Without warning, he shoved the awl deep into a rotten molar. Not knowing what to expect, the death growl emitted from Clem's mouth actually frightened Randy. Letting go the awl, he asked Clem where the money cache was.

Clem was a tough one. He answers, "to my grave with me forever."

"So be it, then it's going there the hard way. The awl found a new nerve, one tooth after the other till he eventually lost all sphincters and smelled like he fell in a privy. He then lost consciousness and his men reacted in a strange way. Clem's screaming and howling had petrified his men. They didn't know Clem had passed out, but still volunteered that the gang's money was buried in the cellar of their house— under a pile of coal.

Randy went to the house with the Mayor and dug it up. The steel box had $8,000 in US Currency. Randy paid off the merchants and gave the mayor $500 for his help. After paying off the merchants, Randy was still holding $5,000 of Clem's money and some $4000 in bounty rewards.

Before leaving town, Randy met with the two victimized ladies. Myra was now a widow and Cindy was a lost seventeen-year-old whose family no longer wanted her home. Myra acknowledged that being after the change of life, she likely would not be pregnant. However, Cindy could be a different matter. Myra would not abandon Cindy in either case.

When Myra was asked what she could do to support herself and Cindy, the answer was housekeeping and cooking. Randy had an idea. He escorted Myra to Butch's Diner and met with Butch's widow. The diner and the furnished apartment upstairs were for sale for $2,300. With Myra's surprised endorsement, Randy purchased the business and apartment on the spot. Randy left $1,000 in Myra's bank account to guarantee operational finances.

Randy then returned to Wichita Falls for rest and relaxation. His reputation was being established as well as building a fund to help victims of violent crimes.

***

CHAPTER 6

CHASING MARAUDERS

Things were quiet in Wichita Falls and Randy was enjoying the down time. One day a man showed up during his dinner at the hotel restaurant. The well-dressed man introduced himself as Stanley Cosby, President of the Community Bank. Once asked to join Randy, Mr. Cosby started with his story.

"You come highly recommended by Sheriff Samuels and Marshall McDonald. I'm in need of a private security force. My bank is holding large amounts of cash for the well-advertised cattle auction next week. I was hoping to get help from our lawmen, but that is not to be for a multitude of reasons. They tell me that you would be capable of protecting my bank during work hours until the auction."

"Why during just work hours and why now? What is the new threat that you're not mentioning?"

"Fair enough, I will come clean. During work hours, the vault is open, or someone is working who can open the locked vault. After closing, even dynamite or fire would not affect the vault—so robbery is impossible after closing. Now the daytime threat comes from banks east of here. I have been warned that the Burdog gang is heading west and will likely try to rob my bank. These are violent criminals that manage to kill at least one clerk during their robberies. My clerks are worried and are considering not coming to work. I admit, I'm also worried."

"Do you honestly believe that I can reassure your workers and thwart a robbery without injury to the help or customers?"

"Yes sir, with the right man, I do. And the marshal and sheriff agree that you are that man. The bank opens Monday morning and the auction is Saturday. If there is a robbery and you capture or kill some outlaws, you will have their bounty and I will also pay you $500 today, should you agree to take the job. Please!"

"Very well, I'll be there by opening time. I will be one of your clerks armed with shotguns and will stay till the Burdog gang hits the bank or the auction starts."

"Great, I'll have a company shirt, vest and visor to match the other clerks."

That weekend, Randy went to several gun shops till he found what he wanted. A new 12-gauge shotgun with mule ear hammers. He had the stock changed to a pistol grip, the barrel cut down to the fore-end wood, the hinge sanded down to allow the barrels to fall open, and the chambers polished to ease chucking of spent shells. The shotgun matched his own sawed-off shotgun in the same gauge.

While waiting for the altered sawed-off shotgun, Randy went to Sheriff McDonald's office to look at wanted posters. It took some time but found several wanted posters on the Burdog gang. The leader was nicknamed Mad Dog because of his violent treatment of ranchers in particular. Mad Dog had a $2,000 bounty and the gang members all had $750 per man. The entire gang was wanted dead or alive because of the carnage they had spread across Texas.

Randy asked the sheriff, "why haven't the Texas Rangers been after this evil gang."

"Because, they are busy fighting the Apaches in South Texas. Until the Apache depredations are stopped, and the Indians are sent to different reservations, they will not be available for assistance anywhere in Texas. For now, lawmen and bounty hunters will have to hold the fort, so to speak."

***

Monday arrived and Randy entered the bank with two sawed-off shotguns. The clerks and President Cosby welcomed Randy. Randy changed the setup of the bank to include a cordoned-off line to one clerk on the left and another cordoned-off line to the right-hand clerk. Randy was in the center counter marked closed where he sat working on a ledger. With the white clerk's shirt, black vest and green visor, he looked the part. However, under the ledger were two loaded double barrel sawed-off shotguns loaded with lethal #3 Buckshot. With everyone ready, the bank doors were opened for business.

The first day was uneventful with business at a regular pace. The second day, Randy was getting bored and started reading his Swanson and Harnell dime novels. He thought it strange how these bounty hunters handled bank robberies, and one method was very similar to the set up prepared in this bank. The one thing he kept wondering about was why the Burdog gang always shot a clerk. As he watched President Cosby open the vault, the answer came to him. By shooting a clerk, the clerk or officer responsible for the vault will not hesitate to open it in the face of a real employee threat. With that in mind, he would be aware that any clerk was at risk and planned to react accordingly.

By closing time, there were only two customers remaining in the right-hand lane when Randy heard the hoof beats of several horses. Looking thru the bank's bay window, he saw several men in the saddle as four were stepping onto the boardwalk and heading for the front doors.

Randy put his right hand on the shotgun's pistol grip and his left hand on the other's fore-end piece. The four men entered and drew their guns and yelled out, "this is a holdup." Randy saw the lead man point his gun at the right lane clerk and as he pulled back the pistol's hammer, Randy reacted. He pulled out the right-hand shotgun and shot the outlaw in the face. As he fell to the floor, his gun discharged and ended up shooting his partner in the foot.

Randy continued shooting and after the first shotgun was shot out, he automatically went to his other shotgun and shot the other two outlaws. With three robbers on the floor and one who had been blown out of the bank's doors, the outside outlaws realized their robbery attempt had been foiled. Mad Dog yells out, "we're done, let's get out of here."

As Randy stepped outside, the outlaws were at a full gallop out of town. Randy had reloaded one shotgun and decided to shoot both barrels at the escaping gang. He was out of lethal range, but still in range to cause some painful damage and the resultant impacts hit several of their targets.

As Marshal McDonald arrived on the scene, Randy says, "Marshal, please clean up the mess because I'm going after the remainder of the gang."

Randy ran to the mercantile and asked the owner to get his trail food order ready. Rushing to the livery, the hostler helped him saddle his horse, packhorse with paniers, and his guns. With Rocky at his side, he stopped to pick up his trail order of canned goods, beef jerky and coffee. By the time he was on the trail tracking the gang he was at least an hour behind the remaining Burdog gang.

The Burdog gang pushed their horses for

two hours before resting and watering the horses. While waiting, Mad Dog tells his men, "robbing banks is getting too dangerous. Some gunfighter was waiting for us and it cost us four good men. Time for us to change our target. There is a cattle auction this weekend, and the auctioneer will be visiting nearby ranches to buy cattle at a discount. We saw him and four cowhands driving some 100 prime steers a few miles back. That means that the ranchers will have some cash available in their ranches. We will follow the cattle tracks to that ranch that made the sale and get some easy money. Now mount up and let's ride."

Arriving at the Bar S Ranch, the gang left their horses on the access road and walked to the ranch house. As they rushed the rear door, they found the elderly rancher and his wife having lunch. Mad Dog demands, "I know you just sold some cattle, so you have some cash handy. Give it to me."

"No way, and if you shoot us my cowhands on the range will be here in minutes."

Mad Dog orders his man standing next to

the elderly wife, "slap her around a bit." The outlaw slaps her hard and the lady fell to the floor.

"You might as well shoot me; cause I'm not giving you money."

Mad Dog was getting furious, he pulls out his hunting knife and drives it into the rancher's shoulder.

The elderly man drops to his knees as the knife is pulled out. Mad Dog then says, "if you don't give it up, I'll put this knife in your wife's ear."

The Burdog gang left with $2,000 in US currency. That night they traveled some 30 miles and finally set up camp around midnight.

Meanwhile, Randy followed the gang's tracks till he came upon a herd of steers driven to the auction. Randy had trouble keeping on the tracks since they were mixed with the herd of steers and cowhands. By darkness, the tracks went to an access road and stopped. Randy realized what had happened and knew the rancher and his family were in trouble.

Stepping onto the ranch-house porch, he

knocked at the front door. The door opened with an elderly man holding a shotgun. Randy realized he had been shot. When he introduced himself as being a bounty hunter after the gang who had just attacked them, Randy was invited in. Randy attended to the man's wound, cleaned it and applied carbolic acid to prevent infection, bandaged it and made a sling for his arm.

The rancher said, "that gang robbed us of $2,000. That's the entire income we needed to live another year and pay our bills. Now we are in trouble and cannot pay our mortgage to the Community Bank or buy food."

Randy simply said, "sir, I will capture this gang, dead or alive, and will return your money. Keep checking with the bank president, Mr. Cosby, for a bank transfer in your name, which is?"

"Ben and Emma Wheelhouse, and your name is?"

"Randy McWain."

***

Meanwhile at the Burdog camp, Mad Dog divided the $2,000 between himself and his six men. "Well boys, that was an easy take without risks. The road to Amarillo is about 200 miles long and there are small ranches or homesteaders along the way that have cash stashed away since there are not always banks handy. We are not stopping in any town till we get to Amarillo. We will steal money, food, ammunition, whiskey, and even horses if necessary. We can even use some of the wives for our pleasure. By the time we arrive in Amarillo, we'll all have several thousand dollars. At that point we need to decide if we disband, and go different ways, or move north as a gang to the Indian Nations to let the law cool off."

Randy continued on the main road heading west-northwest. It was a trail of carnage. He couldn't catch up with the gang because he had to help the victims of their depredations. Some rancher and homesteader men were tortured, shot and even murdered. The wives were beaten and raped in front of their husbands. It became a trail of tears and mayhem. Randy did what he could to bandage the injured, reassure the ladies and even bring some shot up victims to the nearest doctor. He also buried the dead.

One thing was always true, when he left, he had done everything he could to help the victims. Plus, he left with their names, the bank they did business with or the nearest lawman, and the amount of money, food and goods they had lost. He always left his name and an access thru Sheriff Wilcox in Childress. When leaving the victims, he promised everyone that he would provide complete restitution for their losses.

After being on the road some two weeks, he tallied the figures in his log book. The gang had hit 10 ranches and 5 homesteads. They had raped 10 women and killed four men. The financial losses amounted to nearly $22,000. Randy kept looking at all the statistics and realized why this gang would never be caught by the law. They were attacking targets that were at least 20 miles apart and so lawmen, if available, would only know of the victims in their jurisdiction. By the time lawmen investigated the crimes, the culprits were long gone. This only increased his determination to exterminate this evil band from the earth.

Meanwhile, the Birdog gang was camped on the Amarillo outskirts. Mad Dog allowed two men at a time to go into town for entertainment. The problem was that the first two never returned the next day as scheduled. So, a scout was sent to see where they were. The scout came back with the news that their friends had been arrested trying to hold up a gun shop. Mad Dog did not take the news well, especially when he found out that a woman, by the name of Amy Boudreau, had captured his men at gunpoint. After a few days, the gang found the ranch where the Boudreau's lived and decided to kidnap or kill this woman in revenge.

***

Meanwhile after the kidnapping, Randy, carefully loaded the Boudreau's in the wagon with Rocky and a bag of Amy's clothing/personal effects. He trailed his two horses behind the wagon and headed to town. After leaving the

Boudreau's at Doc Cavanaugh's office, Randy rode the wagon to Sheriff Gusfield's office.

After introductions were made, Randy provided a detailed history of the past two weeks that had started with the bank robbery attempt in Wichita Falls. After reviewing Randy's log book, Sheriff Gusfield said, "Two members of this gang were captured a week ago by Amy and she was paid the bounty. Since then, I have received the wanted posters on the remaining members of this gang. Mad Dog has a $2,000 reward and all the remaining gang members have a $750 reward on their heads. The four dead ones at the bank were worth $3,000 and the remaining five are worth $3750."

"That's a fortune, if you are lucky to survive. The risks dealing with this gang are very high. May I suggest that you concentrate your efforts in rescuing Amy and forget about capturing these dangerous killers."

"I can't do that sheriff. I promised over 20 victims that I would avenge their dead and return their money and belongings. My word is my life and I will not break it."

After loading up with supplies, Randy decided to return to the Boudreau ranch to pick up the tracks. After being on the trail for an hour, it became clear that the gang was heading north to the Indian Nations. Randy surmised that they must feel the pressure of being hunted by lawmen or bounty hunters. The need to hide in the Indian Nations was strong--ironically with pockets full of money and no place to spend it.

The Indian Nations were 100 miles north by cross country. With a hostage they would not travel by road. The question in Randy's mind was how long they would keep Amy as a serviceable hostage for their pleasure vs. torturing and killing her for revenge. With Mad Dog and his trail of depredations, anything was possible.

Being at least six hours behind the gang, Randy decided that he needed to push his horses and even travel at night if he wanted to catch up with them by tomorrow.

***

BOOK THREE

AMY AND RANDY

CHAPTER 7

RESCUING AMY

Randy was reluctantly pushing his horses because he was aware, that when darkness fell, it would be very dark with a tiny crescent moon for light. With only water stops whenever a water source was encountered, Randy kept following the tracks till sunset. When he could no longer see the tracks, he stopped and stepped off his horse. Rocky kept sniffing the ground as if he could not identify a scent other than men and horses. That is when Randy had a flash of an idea.

Randy went to his paniers and pulled out the bag of Amy's clothes he had picked out from her bedroom. Most of the clothes had come from the clean dresser, except for her denim britches. The only pair he could quickly locate was a worn pair which he added to the bag. Randy pulled out the pants, opened the waist button, and presented them to Rocky.

Rocky took a good sniff and let out a loud sneeze. He then pawed his nose which Randy didn't understand the significance. Rocky started sniffing the tracks and it became clear he picked up a new scent. Randy said, "track them down, slowly boy."

For hours, Rocky lead the way and for unknown reasons, never lost the scent. The traveling was intentionally slow to avoid gopher or prairie dog holes. Periodically, Rocky would get ahead out of sight. Randy would duplicate a unique song bird tune and Rocky would stop and sit on his haunches waiting for the slow poke horses. With the minimal light from the crescent moon, Randy could see the look on Rocky's face saying, "come along you guys."

Meanwhile, several miles ahead, Mad Dog stopped and set up camp. After the boys started a fire, one of the toadies pulled Amy off her horse, and as her feet hit the ground, her nails scraped the outlaw's face and tore open one eyeball. The man screamed out and was about to cut Amy's throat, when Mad Dog stepped in and punched Amy in the face. Amy was knocked out and Mad Dog said, "tie her spread eagle to the ground and rip her dress off, I'm going to be the first to take her for what she did to my two men." As Mad Dog was about to attack Amy, she opened her eyes and said, "before you do that, better take a good look at me. That blood between my legs is because I have a terrible and untreatable infection that you'll catch. Your manhood will turn red, swell, develop painful bleeding blister and eventually you won't be able to pee, which will kill you." Mad Dog took a step back and started to pull his pants back up and walked away. "Well boys, leave her tied there, and let's think about this over some whiskey, heh."

Hours later, suddenly Rocky stopped and was sniffing the air. Randy finally caught a slight smell of camp smoke. He tied his horses to the nearest mesquite bush and put his backpack shotgun on and started to walk quietly towards the camp.

Getting close to camp, the outlaws were all "out drunk." Randy contemplated how to deal with this problem. He had three choices. The first was a middle of the night frontal assault with his shotgun and Rocky, while the outlaws were all drunk. The second, was to wait till daylight and start picking them off with his long-range scoped rifle. The problem with these two attacks was that Mad Dog could kill the hostage during such attacks.

Then Randy thought of what Sheriff Gusfield had said about rescuing the girl and forget about fighting such a dangerous gang at this time. Randy thought that this was a wise choice, since he could always return and hunt this gang again. They were so violent that no other lawman or bounty hunter would every take them on.

Randy put his shotgun in his backpack and started sneaking into camp. With the camp fire light, he spotted where the girl was and realized she was either asleep or unconscious and tied to the ground in a spread-eagle fashion. Getting to the girl, suddenly he froze. The girl started responding, looked at Randy and said, "stop gawking at me, haven't you ever seen a naked woman before?"

"No ma'am, and please whisper. I'm here to rescue you. As he started cutting her restraints, he added, "and I was not gawking, I was admiring a beautiful body—that be all ma'am. Now, can you walk?"

"I don't know, help me stand to see if I can."

Randy helped her up, being cautious where he put his hands on a naked woman. Once standing, she slowly started falling. Randy put one arm under her legs and one in her back and said, "put you hand around my neck and I'll carry you to my horse."

Randy started walking with his load. After some distance, Amy said, "who are you and why are you risking your life to rescue me."

Carrying a hundred pound of dead weight for 200 yards, Randy knew he couldn't waste any energy talking, so he bluntly blurted out, "because I'm going to marry you, now be quiet before I trip and throw you in a ditch."

Getting to his horses, he considered placing Amy in the saddled horse and he would ride the packhorse behind the paniers. When he placed Amy in the saddle, it was clear that she would fall out and likely kill herself. Instead, Randy got up on the saddled horse and held Amy with his left arm and hand as he encouraged her to hold on to the saddle horn. They traveled two hours in this fashion and Randy could tell Amy was getting stronger and more able to be more independent in holding on.

As instructed, Amy had kept her mouth shut, since she felt secure sitting in front of this man. Eventually, she said, "it's not for modesty since you've seen every inch of my body, but I'm freezing to death. Could I get covered with a coat or a blanket?"

"Sorry, I've been too occupied to get away from that gang. Of course," as Randy stopped the horses, helped Amy down, went rummaging in the paniers and came back with a shirt, britches and shoes. Randy added his own wool shirt to top her cotton shirt.

Amy was surprised to see her own clothes. She was about to start asking questions when Randy said, "no time for questions, let's get back on the trail. They then mounted and continued their traveling back to Amarillo. By daylight, Randy decided to stop and set up camp. He realized that they would not be able to outrun these killers, so, the answer was to make a firm stand. He had to convince them that it would be to their advantage to let go the hunt and escape with their lives and money.

Dismounting, Amy asked, "we've been pushing all night, now that its daylight, why are we stopping?"

Randy explained why they had to make a definitive stand. He said, "look at that rise behind us. That's 300 yards. I have a scoped long-range rifle that will reach out there and cause them some serious damage. I hope to get them off our tail. I'll set my rifle on that boulder and start watching for them to arrive. Would you start a fire so we can cook breakfast.

Once things settle down, we'll talk since there is much you need to know. Ok?"

Randy had his 50X binoculars and was looking for a dust cloud that would signify their presence. Amy started a fire, added the cooking grate, a coffee pot and started to heat up bacon, canned beans and canned potatoes. The coffee was ready first and Amy brought a cupful to Randy. When breakfast was ready, she brought Randy and her own plateful, and joined him on his watch.

After enjoying a hot meal in quietude, Amy finally asked, "what's your name, who are you and why did you risk your life to save me?"

"Well once you know all those answers, we'll know each other and the courtship will come to an end, heh?" Seeing Amy frustrated to hear his sarcastic answer he added, "Ok, sorry, here goes."

My name is Randy McWain age 22, raised in Childress Texas, and worked as a deputy sheriff in that town. For over a year, I've been on my own, with Rocky, as a bounty hunter. I had been on the Burdog's trail since their bank robbery in Wichita Falls. I've been on the northwest trek following the depredations of this evil group of men. They have killed four men, raped a dozen of women, and stole at least $22,000 from their victims."

"Now getting to you, I followed this gang to your home. Your mother was unconscious. and your dad had been shot in the shoulder. There was no one else around and so I loaded your parents in a wagon and brought them to your local doctor, Doc Cavanaugh. Before I left your dad, he offered me $10,000 if I brought you back alive and unharmed. Now I figured if your father was offering a small fortune for you, that you must be some special person. That's why I risked my life to save you, not because of the money. Now only time will confirm if your dad was correct or just emotional."

Amy moved closer, reeled her right hand back and smacked Randy across the face with the flat of her hand. She then exclaims, "that was for your so called 'admiring my body.'" She then leans into his face and plants a soft kiss on his reddened cheek saying, "and that's for saving my life. Thank you for me and my parents."

***

While still watching the backtrail for a dust cloud, Randy asked Amy, "tell me about your upbringing and what have you been doing since arriving at legal age?"

My early upbringing was a happy time. I was born late in my parents lives and I was loved to pieces. As a young woman, I followed my mother's talents in designing and sewing clothing. Plus, my father allowed me to learn about guns from one of the cowhands. By the age of 18. I got a job working at the Westland Gun Shop and learned the art of selling and repairing guns. My other job was working for Harvey Samuel's saddlery shop making harnesses and holsters."

"Before I left Amarillo, Sheriff Gusfield mentioned that you had captured two of Mad dog's men. How did that happen?"

"The two idiots pulled a gun on Mr. Westland to rob him. I just pulled out my Wesley Bulldog and shot the gun out of his hand. The bounty reward was a total shock to me. The $1500 was greater than my year's salary at the gun shop and saddlery."

As Randy was listening to Amy, he spotted a dust cloud. Randy handed his binoculars to Amy and started spotting in his Win 76 rifle scope. As the five riders appeared on top of the rise, Randy spotted one of the riders and squeezed off a shot. The rider went over backwards over the horse's rump and landed on his face. The other riders pulled up. One man stepped down from his horse to check his down friend, as Randy shot at the man's feet. The outlaw quickly mounted his horse as the leader ordered his four men back below the top of the rise, out of the shooter's sight.

Amy was watching the going's on and said, "you missed the second outlaw, heh?"

"No, that was a warning shot. They already knew I could hit any one of them if I wanted to. Right now, they are over the rise, trying to decide what their next move should be. Let's wait."

"That shooter has a scoped long-range rife and likely a bounty hunter. I suggest we abandon the hunt for that woman. Let's get out of here and head for the Indian Nations."

"But boss, Slim is lying over the rise with $4,000 in his pocket and I'm going back to get it."

"Dude, now I know why they call you Bubba, you're an idiot. If you're going back to get Slim's money, then leave me your own $4,000, since where you'll be going, you won't need any cash." After the gang thought about their options, they all agreed and turned their horses towards the north to the Indian Nations.

Randy and Amy were still watching when both picked up a dust cloud heading north. Amy said, "nice work Randy. You stopped them and guaranteed our safety."

"Don't count your chickens before they hatch, they could be circling around to attack our camp. Let's get on our horses and ride to check that downed outlaw. At the same time, we'll use our scopes to verify we don't have visitors in camp."

Randy checked the dead outlaw's pockets and found $4,029 in US Currency. In the horse's saddlebags was a Remington 41 caliber derringer with a box of ammo. The saddle had a pommel holster and a scabbard with a new Win 73 rifle in the new caliber 44-40. The gunbelt had a cross-draw holster holding a new Colt also in 44-40 like the rifle. As Randy was about to leave, he verified that their camp didn't have any visitors. Suddenly, Amy says, "wait a minute."

Amy walks over to the dead outlaw and pulls off his boots saying, "these look new and are my size. They are better for riding than the day shoes you brought me, heh." Randy just rode off, trailing the outlaw's horse, and raising his eyebrows in surprise and satisfaction.

Back at camp, Randy needed to make plans. "Look ma'am, you've had two concussions within 24 hours. I suggest we rest the day, get a good night's sleep and ride back to Amarillo in the morning. What do you think?"

"Ok with me as long as you drop the 'ma'am, my mother is a ma'am, my name is Amy.

Secondly, I get to use your bar of soap so I can clean up at the stream."

"Certainly, here's the lye soap and bring Rocky with you for protection."

Some time later, Rocky comes back without Amy and goes to the packsaddle looking for something. Randy realized what Rocky was looking for. He grabs a blanket and starts walking to the stream. "Is this what you sent Rocky for?"

Amy was in a deep pool up to her shoulders in water. She says, "Yes, please throw it to me."

"Uh, if we miss our shot, you'll have nothing to dry yourself off with."

"Right, step into the stream and hand it to me then."

"I'm not getting these boots wet; they'll shrink and be too tight!"

"Oh for 'pete-sakes,' hand it to me!" As Amy starts walking out of the deep pool towards Randy, exposing a full-frontal view of her nakedness.

Amy adds, "shut your mouth Randy, the

bugs are going to crawl in. Now get—so I can dry up and get dressed with modesty.

For the remainder of the day, Amy and Randy enjoyed reading the two bounty hunter novels by Harnell and Swanson. For dinner, Randy made a beef stew out of canned beef and vegetables while Amy made hoe cakes out of corn meal and bacon grease. Dessert consisted of canned peaches and coffee. The evening was getting chilly and Amy was glad to use Randy's winter coat. With two bedrolls on the ground, it was difficult to share one blanket. Despite their attempt in sharing it and beefing up the fire, both were getting cold. Finally, Randy said, "Amy this is not working. Snuggle your back to mine so we can share body heat as well as the blanket."

Amy took off Randy's winter coat and draped it over both of them then pushed her back to Randy's. With the blanket snuggled to her neck, Amy had a smile on her face as she fell asleep. Randy was first to awaken as daylight came. On opening his eyes, he found Amy half crawled onto his chest and snoring loudly. To complete the scene, Rocky was laying on top of the blanket and snuggled against Amy. Randy eased out from the winter coat and blanket and got up to go to the bushes. Not risking going back to the bedroll, he started breakfast.

After Rocky came to smell the cooking bacon, Amy awoke and rushed to the bushes. Upon, her return, Randy handed her a cup of coffee and she said, "boy, I slept like a log once I warmed up. Did I snore and waken you?"

"Yes ma'am, I mean Amy. But I'm not sure who was worse, you or the dog, as Rocky cocked his head sideways. Rocky got a full bowl of porridge and beef jerky for breakfast. After a welcomed breakfast of beans, fried potatoes and bacon with coffee, Randy started picking up the camp. Amy interrupted him and asked him to sit and talk.

"Last night, I couldn't fall asleep and kept thinking of the bounty hunter book I had read yesterday. To get to the point, I want to go after the Burdog gang, and I want to become a bounty hunter. Would you take me along and teach me?"

"Lady, are you nuts? Do you realize what you're asking? Bounty hunting is one of the most dangerous professions. It requires countless days on the trail dealing with cold, rain, snow, blistering sun and the chance of an ambush every day. It requires you to be able to kill a man in self-defense or out of necessity. The odds can be against you in a gunfight. Worse of all, you are risking your life to remove these psychopathic villains from circulation, and the public and lawmen look down at you in return for your efforts. In addition, it's not right for a man and woman to be partners in this profession. Ridiculous, totally ridiculous. Mount up so I can bring you back to your folks."

"Randy, your negative reasons are feeble. You are digging a hole, and every word you say digs you deeper. Now let me tell you why I would be an ideal partner and how we can proceed safely in this profession. A lawman knows what he can expect from his deputies as I will clarify how you can depend on me."

I'm very proficient with the rifle and pistol. I can outdraw most men and I'm accurate. I will not be an executioner but will not put our lives in danger to bring a murderer to hang. We can discuss the different ways to implement a takedown but will accept your decision as final and will do my best to always have your back."

"You may think that a female partner will require luxuries. That is ridiculous and only time will convince you otherwise—you'll never hear me complain about hardships. As far as being in the saddle all day, I'll match your stamina any day. This issue of a man traveling with a female partner, I will maintain a modest decorum with you. I won't pull a nudity caper like I did at the stream yesterday. Now when the goings get tough, you can count on me. I will take a bullet for you any day. That's the kind of partner I'd be."

"I must be getting soft or old. Something tells me I should give you a try. Under one condition, that you keep your female attributes under modest control. I can't be riding a horse all day in distress while bouncing on a saddle. I have to be on my game, and not walking around in a semi aroused state all day."

"Agree."

"After a few weeks of training, we'll share the bounty rewards in a ratio of 70-30%. Only time and experience will determine whether the partnership will last. Our first hunt will be after the Burdog gang—for restitution and justice."

***

CHAPTER 8

THE FIRST HUNT

Before we get on the trail, I want you proficient in the use of certain firearms. Let me see what you can do with a Colt pistol and a Win 73 rifle. Amy used his gunbelt and added the outlaw's cross draw holster to the belt. She demonstrated her fast draw from either holster and her accuracy with point and shoot. She then did free standing speed-rifle shooting with a Win 73. Her proficiency more than satisfied Randy.

Now I have a sawed-off shotgun with a backpack. This is the firearm that is your go-to gun in a gun fight. I will show you how to draw it, cock it and fire from the hip. The other rifle you need to learn is the scoped Win 76 long-range firearm. We will spend the necessary days practicing these two firearms. In addition, we will discuss the different gunfighting scenarios we are likely to encounter. After that, you'll learn bounty hunting thru living experiences."

For the remainder of the day, they practiced the proper use of the sawed-off shotgun. Amy could see how deadly such a weapon could be. After three hours she was able to point and shoot a 10-yard target on the run. Shooting long-range required the use of a solid rest and mathematical ciphering to adjust the scope at different elevations between 100 and 400 yards. The recoil and report took some getting use to but eventually she was placing a fatal hit on a man size target at 400 yards. Again, Randy was pleased with her quick learning abilities and a positive attitude towards becoming proficient with new firearms.

That evening, sitting by the fire, Randy started presenting several scenarios and described how to handle each one as safely as possible. They included when and how to use Rocky, how to cross country track, handling a cabin siege, arresting criminals in saloons, how to spot an ambush, how to even the numbers of outlaws in their favor, how to make an outlaw divulge secrets without physical evidence of torture, how to visit with lawmen and review reward posters, how to go undercover, and many others worth mentioning.

For sleeping arrangements, the persisting cold forced them to share the winter coat and blanket. Back spooning started the night, but they both knew the positions would change like they did the night before. In the morning, Amy was up first and actually started the coffee and breakfast before Randy and Rocky were awake.

After breakfast, Randy cleaned the dishes and then resumed his discussion of the different scenarios. By late morning, he asked Amy if she had any questions.

"Yes, only two. In a gunfight, am I your backup or do we each act independently?"

"Independently, but with some order. Let's use a theoretical example. Leaving Rocky out of a gunfight, let's say we have no choice but for us to go against five gunfighters. With each of our shotguns out and ready to fire, if you are on my left, I would expect you to put down the two men on the left when you see them start their draw. I would be responsible for the two on the right. That leaves the center outlaw which will usually be the leader or the fastest gun. In this case, with one outlaw standing, we both drop our shotguns and draw/fire on the last man standing. Even if the outlaw gets a shot off, the other person will put the outlaw down, even if one of us is shot. The one thing in our favor is that the center outlaw often will catch a few pellets from the shotgun blasts which tends to throw off his timing—but never count on such an advantage."

"The second question, "what are your ethical standards regards to shooting a criminal in the back?"

"Rarely should that ever happen. The dead men I bring in will be shot in the front and I always try to bring as many in alive as dead. Yet, I think I mentioned this; we will not risk our lives to bring a killer sitting in the saddle. Using judgement, the receiving lawmen prefer to have a man alive to stand trial."

"So as bounty hunters, we are our own boss. Yet, it's customary to visit with lawmen when we arrive in town. That way, if we bring in dead outlaws, the lawman will be more willing to certify their identity and process the bounty reward."

"That's right! Well, what do you say we break camp and do some riding before nightfall while the tracks are still visible.

***

Two hours into the ride, the duo stopped to water their horses and let them crop some grass. Randy replaced the water in the canteens and shared some beef jerky with Amy and Rocky. Randy had forgotten about a woman's need to seek privacy for nature's call. When she returned from the bushes, he said, "If ever you need to stop for nature's call, don't hesitate to alert me."

"Now I saw that you had your pistol in the saddle's pommel holster. That's the thing to do with a cross draw holster which tends to bounce the pistol against the saddle. When we get to town, we'll get you a hip holster with legging strings. Until then, don't go to the bushes with your pistol left in the pommel holster. You always need that gun on your body if you're not riding in the saddle. When your feet hit the ground, the pistol should follow."

"Of course, that will never happen again."

Back on the trail, the ground got rocky and tracking was slow and difficult. To make it worse, it started to rain, and Randy decided to stop and make camp before the downpour started. As soon as they arrived at a decent location, Randy laid a rope between two trees and made a lean-to out of a large tarp. Under the tarp, he started a cooking fire and then took out a tent out of his panniers. With Amy's help, the tent quickly went up. The panniers holding food went into the tent and the saddles went under the tarp. Just as everything was set up, heavy rain started. The air became chilly and Amy used Randy's winter coat, while Randy was wrapped in their only blanket—but with three shirts underneath.

Being warm and dry, coffee made the afternoon bearable. The talk eventually moved onto the Burdog gang. Amy asks, "what do you expect we'll encounter when we meet up with Mad Dog and his toadies."

"They have plenty of money, so I don't believe they will stop to rob or kill. I think they are heading straight to the Indian Nations, where they will lose most lawmen on their tail. Once they settle in the Nations, it will be difficult to root them out. Our only chance is to reach the border Texas towns as soon as possible. If we're lucky, we may find the gang, or part of the gang, spending a few days in saloons with working gals before hiding in the wilderness."

That night, sleeping arrangements were different. They both entered the tent and tightly snuggled onto the bedrolls, winter coat and blanket—Rocky stayed outside under the tarp. The added tent's protection kept the temperature up a bit more than sleeping outside.

Despite this, Amy still managed to roll onto Randy's chest by morning.

The next three days, the weather was mild and sunny. The duo stopped in a small town to replenish their food supply and buy several wool blankets. Amy also picked up a winter jacket and gloves, winter socks, a rain duster, a side buscadero holster for her Colt and replacement shirts and britches.

By late afternoon the third day, they arrived in a border town with several businesses. The horses and Rocky were left in a livery for extra feedings of oats and hay. They walked to the hotel with their shotguns and stepped up to the hotel. Randy paid for one room and signed in as Mr. and Mrs. Cramer. When entering the room, Amy said, "I'm surprised with your strong modesty ethics that you plan to share a room. What is up?"

"This room has a water toilet and running hot water. Enjoy a bath and relax while I visit the local law. I'll explain later."

Walking towards the sheriff's office, Randy sees a special mercantile. He steps in and $500 later left with two small packages. He then walks to the sheriff's office. Upon entering, the sheriff was seen as a rotund white-haired elderly man asleep in his chair. When awakened, he greeted Randy. After introductions, Sheriff Craighead gladly went over reward posters. When Randy saw the poster for Mad Dog, he pulled it out as he noticed the sheriff turning pale.

"Yes, that monster has been in Crane's Saloon now for several days. He appears to have his own crew of miscreants and has managed to send three men to the local doc with bad lacerations. Mr. Crane is besides himself since no one wants to confront this gang."

"Well, my partner and I will be glad to arrest them and bring them to your jail, pending transfer to Amarillo where they would stand trial."

"You may want to reconsider your plans; these are killers who enjoy hurting and killing people!"

"I know, that's why we need to stop them. No one else would ever step up. Besides, my fiancé needs restitution. See you later."

Randy returned to the hotel. Using his key, he unlocked the door and walked in. Amy was standing next to the tub and had a towel wrapped around herself as she was drying her hair with another towel.

Amy adds, "next time, better knock since you could have found me in an immodest condition."

"Sorry, but this is a rush. Mad Dog and crew are in Crane's Saloon. I want you to get all gussied up, so they don't recognize you as the plain-Jane they kidnapped. Don't wear that binder you wear to prevent your upper attributes from bouncing when you're in the saddle. Plus, add some colored powder if you have it and wear your outfit seductively."

"Well I can do this, thanks to my purchases at the last town's mercantile. Give me my saddlebags and go to the livery to get my bag from the panniers. I'll start while you're gone."

Randy returned with the bag and handed it to Amy thru the half- opened water closet door. It seemed like an eternity, but eventually Amy stepped out, fully gussied up. Randy could not believe his eyes; Amy was a shocker. He said, "boy you're a real mole aren't you. You are gorgeous with your tight shirt, cleavage, exaggerated attributes, tight britches, facial rouge, lip paint, Colt at your side and a shotgun on your back. I can just imagine what will happen when you walk in the saloon. Wild, simply wild times are coming!"

"Did I over do it, I thought this is what you wanted?"

"Well, there is no doubt, Mad Dog and crew won't recognize you and that will give us the element of surprise. Now to keep the riffraff off your back, wear this ring." This is what the jeweler called a half 'carrot dimon'—whatever that is, and what do vegetables have to do with white rocks. Anyways, it will show that you are my women and will push most bums away. After all, I wanted you disguised, not advertised, heh."

"What the heck, I'll wear an engagement ring, after-all you said you were going to marry me. For now, we can play the part."

Entering the saloon, Randy and Amy

stepped up to the bar and ordered two beers. As expected, an arrogant smartass came over and squeezed himself between Amy and Randy. "Well honey, where did you come from? Why don't we step outside and have some fun?"

"Sorry fella, see this ring, I'm already spoken for."

"Hell, that don't matter, he don't need to know!"

Randy places his hand behind his neck and says, "You are an idiot." Suddenly, to avoid an outright encounter, Randy pushes the drunk's head down and slams his face onto the bar. The fella was stunned but heard Randy say, "now, quietly walk out of here while you can still walk."

Fortunately, the hub-bub quickly settled down and Amy was left alone to her beer. With a sign from Randy, the duo makes their move to Mad Dog's table.

Standing side by side with shotguns drawn, Randy says, "Mad Dog your trail of misery has come to an end. Stand up all of you, you're all under arrest."

As the four men stood up and turned to face the duo, Mad Dog recognized Amy. "You, again. This time I should kill you."

Knowing that Amy wanted her revenge, Randy decided to goad Mad Dog into making an aggressive move. So, he said, "Mister, you are some ugly dude. You have hair growing out of your ears and nose, have the eyes of a wolf, the teeth of a bear and smell like a buffalo cow in heat. This certainly explains why they call you Mad Dog. You're so ugly that when you fell out of the ugly tree, you must have hit every branch on the way down."

Several of the patrons started laughing till Randy yells out, "I want everyone, except the barkeep, out of here, NOW." Anticipating a gunfight, everyone cleared out. The barkeep, owner Crane, was told to apply the manacles to all four men. As Crane started for the four outlaws, Mad Dog stopped him.

"That's enough, we are not going with you peaceably. There are four of us against you two and we'll likely put you down." That's when things turned to slow motion in Randy's eyes.

All four men went for their guns. Randy and Amy both fired one barrel as their dedicated man was blown onto the floor. As Randy prepared to fire his second barrel, he heard a click from Amy's shotgun. At the same time that Randy fired his second barrel, Amy drew her pistol and fired at Mad Dog's hand as it was lifting his pistol out of the holster.

The bullet impact severed his hand off and Mad Dog went into an immediate state of shock. With the other three men down, Randy wrapped a pigging string around the spraying stub. Randy didn't want Mad Dog to bleed to death, he had a rope waiting for him.

Escorting Mad Dog to the local doc, Randy stayed guard while the doctor finished his work cleaning and suturing the stub. The doc charged $5 and said, "that will likely prevent infection and bleeding till the trial."

That night, as they closed the door to their room, Randy made something very clear. "When I heard the click of a dud shell, I knew you were dead. Then I heard you fire your pistol as I shot off my second shotgun barrel. You never hesitated. It's as if your brain processed the click and started your draw before you realized what was happening. Do you remember how it all happened?"

"Randy, all I knew was that the two men to my left were Mad Dog and his man. According to our agreement, they were my responsibility and I wasn't about to let them shoot us. I will only admit that I was in complete control of my brain and my gun hand. A click on a dud shell can always happen, and I practiced that by adding a dud shell to every box I shot off. A random click every box of 25 shells was the way I practiced the recovery."

"Ok, now to maintain the façade that we are a couple, we now have one room and one bed. How do you want to work things out?"

"Well, we've been on the trail for days, sleeping fully clothed under the stars. Tonight, I'm getting in my chemise and panties and sleeping in a real bed. You are welcome to do the same or sleep on the floor. Afterall, we are allegedly engaged, it's not like we're married. I'm sure I'm not in any danger, heh."

Randy was not about to sleep on the floor. So, he undressed down to his union suit and jumped into bed. Amy came from the water closet, was scantily clad, and jumped under the blankets as Randy could see her fully erect attributes. Despite mother nature, both fell asleep. As usual, morning found Amy sprawled all over Randy. This morning, it was Amy who woke first. As she found herself laying over Randy, she just smiled and rushed to the water closet to do her business and get dressed.

Coming out of the water closet, Randy was dressed and waiting for Amy. Amy approached Randy and handed him the diamond ring. Randy said, "no, keep it on. We need to maintain the couple appearance until we are out of town. Besides, since I'm going to marry you, it will eventually belong to you, heh."

"You keep talking like that and one day I'm going to say yes. Now I'm starved, let's go to breakfast."

Waiting for their meal, the duo did not realize that they were being watched by another table.

"Mr. Whiting, look at that cowgirl on your left. That's a good- looking gal who would add quality to our next shipment to Wichita Falls." "Yes, but she wears a ring and a Colt pistol. I doubt that cowboy would let her go. Way too risky, best we stay with Indian squaws and homesteader wives. For what they are used for, it's all the same."

After breakfast, the duo went to see Sheriff Craighead. "The trial is in two days and the prosecutor would like you to be witnesses. I have already received telegram vouchers totaling almost $5,000 since the rewards went up after their trek of depredations from Wichita Falls. To pay the sheriff for the use of his jail and hopefully the gallows, Randy gave him a bank voucher of $300. "That's way too much Mr. McWain."

"No, besides, I suspect we'll be working together again."

Leaving the office, the duo headed for the bank. Randy gave Amy half of the $5,000 bounty. Amy said, "what happened to the 70-30 ratio you proposed?"

"After seeing you shoot Mad Dog's hand off, you clearly are going to be an equal partner. Besides, when I marry you, I'm going to get it all back anyways, heh."

"Well, being high maintenance, you would certainly need it!"

Amy started her own account with $2,500 as Randy started his own with a total of $6,000. This included the current bounty, four bounties from the bank and one bounty on the trail to turn the Burdog gang away. Randy kept $250 in cash for expenses.

For two days, awaiting the trial, the duo had plenty of time to decide their future. Over a quiet table, sipping on hot coffee, Randy asked Amy what she wanted to do now that Mad Dog was revenged. Amy surprised Randy by saying she had an immediate goal and a long-term plan. Randy asked for more details as they walked back to the hotel.

"My immediate plans involve continuing the bounty hunting trail, for one year, to rid North Texas of as many evil men that no one dares to go after. At the same time, I need to amass a financial base to pursue my lifelong dream of owning my own company, which is my long-term goal."

"Wow that's a tall order. It's a dangerous profession and there's no guarantee you'll survive the year."

"I wasn't planning to do this alone, I want to do this with you 50-50, heh."

"Now you listen to me carefully, I will do this under certain conditions that are not negotiable. The first is that, like a game hunter going where the game is, we go where the outlaws are and that is in the Indian Nations. The second is that my decisions are final, and you'll support me 100%. The third and last is, uh, well, so, heck, will, no more"

"Randy stop talking gibberish."

"The third is, I'm not spending one more unbearable night with you unless you marry me!"

"Damn Randy, I thought you'd never ask. I knew the night you carried my naked body to my horse that I would marry you."

Getting back to the hotel, the duo was barely thru the door when the clothes started coming off and hands started roaming. The two were inept at love making in their own way. They quickly agreed to show each other the things that pleasured themselves. Their passion grew slowly till neither could hold back any longer. They simultaneously consummated their love in a peak of ecstasy.

Finally catching their breaths, Amy said, "to think I wasted years to find the pleasure in loving a man."

"I don't miss what I didn't have, but now that I found this and you, I'm going to enjoy relations and you for years. This is just our beginning."

Amy's hand started roaming and when she found her target, she adds, "I see we're ready again, heh?"

The next morning, they both bathed and changed in clean clothes. Arriving at the sheriff's office, they dragged Sheriff Craighead to the nearest minister and used him as a witness to their marriage. Randy had the wedding bands and to Amy's surprise, the bands matched her diamond ring.

After the wedding, Amy started crying.

When Randy asked her why she was crying, she said, "I never ever realized that I would marry, while on the trail I fell completely captivated by you and I'm so much in love with you that I can't think."

"I know everything was rushed, but it feels right, and I know it's right. We need our own honeymoon before we go to work. So, let's spend a week in the hotel as husband and wife and get to really know each other. Then we'll go to work."

That night, they gladly consummated their marriage after a candlelight dinner served in their honeymoon suite. The next morning, after another roll in the sac, they went to the courthouse for Mad Dog's trial. Randy testified on the evidence of depredations from Wichita Falls to Amarillo. Amy testified that Mad Dog had shot her dad and had kidnapped her after an aggravated assault. The jury was out for ten minutes and found Mad Dog guilty of unforgiveable crimes against humanity. He was sentenced to hang within 24 hours.

After the trial, the duo went to the telegraph

office. Amy sent a telegram to her parents, saying that she had been rescued by Randy, went on the hunt for Burdog, brought Mad Dog down, his crew had been eliminated, she was now married to Randy and would be on the bounty hunting trail for some time but not more than a year.

That same day, the duo went to the jail to see Mad Dog. After applying the manacles, the sheriff went out for lunch and left the duo at work. Randy said, "your life is coming to an end tomorrow. Don't you think it's time to reveal where you have over $20,000. It's time to provide restitution to the many ranchers and homesteaders you robbed and killed.

"I don't care, their loss will keep me in their minds for years to come, ha, ha. ha'ah."

"I guess we have no choice, I'm going to get this information the hard way, even if it takes till morning"

"What are you going to do, beat it out of me?"

"Hell no, I have a better way." With the sheriff gone, Randy opened the cell's door. Amy was left to stand as security in case Mad Dog overpowered Randy. Randy threw Mad Dog to the cot on his back. He jumped on his chest and pried his mouth open. Without any warning, he shoved the awl deep in a rotten molar. Mad Dog went stiff followed by a scream from hell. As Randy was moving the awl, Mad Dog would change his tune to screeches and legs were kicking air.

Amy had never seen such response to pain and had to hold on to the bars to prevent from falling down. Every screech from Mad Dog gave Amy goosebumps and the willies.

When Randy pulled the awl out, he added, "well Mad Dog, that takes care of one molar-the nerve is pretty much shot. However, I count four more bad molars and two bad premolars. Looks like you have six more rounds coming. After that, we'll break some front teeth to expose the nerve and continue with either the awl or a cold-water wash, heh!"

"Go to hell, I'm a dead man anyways."

"Realizing that this was going to be more difficult than anticipated, he decided to send Amy to see the local doctor to get a bottle of a specific liquid. As soon as Amy was out of the jail, he went back to work on Mad Dog. After three ruined molars, Amy arrived. Mad Dog was sweating, had wet himself and was totally spent.

"Now Mad Dog, time to get back to work on you. However, I am willing to offer you an alternative. This is a bottle of laudanum; it has three large doses which will kill the toothaches and keep you happy till your execution. The alternative is hours of more dental torture."

"Mad Dog went silent, kept looking at the bottle and finally said, "Why not. The money means nothing to me, so give me the first dose of laudanum and I'll tell you where the money is>"

"Oh no, let's compromise, a half dose for the location. When I return with the money, you get the other half. Sheriff Craighead will dispense the other two full doses when needed."

"Alright, the money is in the bank's vault in a private safety deposit box under the name of Horace Samuel Burden, my real birth name. I'll sign a release and provide a box number to give you access."

Randy, Amy and Sheriff Craighead got access to the safety deposit box and found $24,000 in currency. They took the log that Randy had generated from his weeks on the trail of depredations and were able to divide the list into four groups. One group would receive a telegraph voucher for the funds, a second would get their money thru a bank transfer and another would have a hand delivery by the local lawman. Only a few had no choice but to get their funds from a local mercantile owner. The total distributions came up to $20,488. The balance of $3,500 was distributed to the widows of the killed ranchers.

After their honeymoon week, the duo had a long meeting with Sheriff Craighead regarding his knowledge of outlaws in the Indian Nations. Over a long dinner in the hotel's restaurant, Sheriff Craighead was found to be very knowledgeable about where the outlaws could be found.

"Outlaws swarm to the southern border of the Indian Nations on a year-round basis. They have two lodging choices. In warm weather, most set up camp with tarps and tents and buy their supplies in the trading posts. This is expensive but then they have a lot of money to spend on food and whiskey. The second choice is to pay to stay in an Indian camp, especially in the winter. They pay a monthly fee at the end of each month which includes a heated teepee, two meals a day, and squaw services but at an extra charge. The cost is high, but the Indians use this money in the trading posts to pay for meat and dry goods to support their tribe."

"Now the problem is how do you two determine who is hiding in the Nations that have a bounty on their head."

"No idea yet."

"Well I am the answer—for a small fee. Being a border town, I get telegram notices of who is heading towards town. Once they get here, they quickly move to the Nations. Were you to check with me periodically, I would tell you who to look for, and provide some unique individual features to help you identify them."

Amy asks, "how do we find where these

outlaws are hiding, a private camp or with the Indians."

"You'll have to watch the trading posts as far who is coming or going. The trading post owners cannot risk helping you, you'll have to do your own tracking of suspicious customers. Now as far as those hiding with Indians, you need to make contact with a well-known Cheyenne chief by the name of Chief Blue Sky. He's against his people harboring outlaws and is willing to help bounty hunters— especially those wearing a lawman's badge, which I know you own one, heh!"

Randy says, "deal, how about 10% of the bounties, dead or alive."

"Way more than needed, but it's a deal. Plus, I will hold the living in my jail till I make arrangements to transfer them for trial and sentencing. The dead will be buried after identification."

A week later, they started preparing for their work. A large tent was bought, and the panniers were filled with food and several changes of clothes, including cold weather items. It was fall and the evenings were getting chilly. These extra clothing items and tent were added to the third pannier.

The new items requiring the fourth pannier were animal traps, especially medium size bear traps—made to hold a man's leg at boot tops and inflict damage and pain. A last addition was an extra packhorse to haul the last two panniers.

When they were ready to leave, they decided to start watching several trading posts and look for outlaws. The duo had a leather satchel full of wanted posters provided by Sheriff Craighead. It was not yet winter, so checking out Indian camps would wait for colder weather. For now, private outlaw camps were their best bet.

Riding a full day and covering 25 miles brought the duo to a chosen base camp they would use while watching trading posts.

***

CHAPTER 9

INDIAN NATION

Outlaw and Cheyenne Camps

The trading post was called Rocky Creek Trading and was owned and operated by Ezra McCullock. This was a muscular and short burly man wearing a pistol who appeared very capable of taking care of any problem from outlaws or Indians. The duo was walking throughout the store looking at the items for sale. There were supplies that would satisfy either outlaws or Indians.

The outlaws wanted coffee, whiskey and canned foods ready to eat. They especially liked canned beans, potatoes, beef stew, and ham. Bacon and raw steaks were the only meats they bought fresh. The only food they would prepare was hoe cakes made from bacon fat and corn meal. The available fresh vegetables were potatoes and onions. Occasionally, an outlaw camp would have a cook that would be looking for different ingredients and foods. It was clear that this trading post had either canned goods, dry goods, salt, sugar and bacon brought in by freight wagons from North Texas. The fresh beef came from the owner butchering cattle from his own herd.

The Indians were buying different items. They wanted sugar, flour, corn meal, corn on the cob, beans by the bags, potatoes, onions, coffee, and barrels of molasses. Meat was purchased by paying dearly for living cattle. They had no taste for canned foods or for pork products including bacon. As in older times, McCullock traded with the Indians for their pelts, but ended up taking advantage of the desperate Indians. The Indians knew they fared better with gold or paper money to get their food.

The other supplies provided by McCullock

included clothing for men, bedrolls, blankets, tents, ammunition, pans, pots, cooking utensils, tobacco, cheroots and whiskey.

After walking around and making a mental list of the store's supplies, Randy said, "Amy, why don't you pick up what we need while I talk to the owner."

"Ok, but it's going to be mostly canned foods, fresh potatoes and onions, and bacon to supplement our supplies. There is also beef roasts from his recent butchering that looks good"

Introducing himself to McCullock, Randy said, "I'm certain you are wondering why a couple is here. Well, there is no denying it, we are bounty hunters. I know you cannot talk about your customers for fear of losing your store or your life. However, if ever some outlaws threaten you, you can find us camped upstream a couple of miles to the east."

"I'm glad to hear you are staying nearby, being the only 'civilian' trading with outlaws and Indians. I'll keep your offer in mind."

The duo decided to start watching who was

coming to the trading post. Amy was watching the eastern route into the post, whereas, Randy was watching the western route. After a week, it was clear that the eastern traffic consisted of freight wagons bringing in supplies. Also, several homesteaders were coming to trade their products for needed supplies. The western route consisted of individuals coming in with packhorses and leaving with their panniers full. These individuals were outlaws that matched the wanted posters.

Amy suggested, "let's abandon the eastern route, it's clear that the outlaws are west of the trading posts."

"I agree, we'll watch the trading post and start following the next suspicious hombre."

That night, after dinner, they had a visitor. It was an Indian woman. As she arrived, she said, "Ezra talk, you come now."

The duo saddled their horses and followed her to the trading post. Ezra greeted them and said, "thank you for coming, this is my squaw wife, Red Flower. I asked you to come because I'm having trouble with an outlaw gang. Two men came to get supplies, and for the third time they were leaving without paying. This last time, I told them that their credit was over $50 and if they didn't pay, they would have to take their business elsewhere.

"How did that go."

"Not well, instead of paying me, they started beating me. Thanks to Red Flower, who pulled out the shotgun, they left with their supplies but made it clear that they would return with their partners and clean me out."

"How can we help?"

"I expect they'll be back tomorrow with their gang to wipe me out. These are dangerous outlaws with prices on their heads. Could I hire you as security guards. I'm certain that they all have hefty bounties on the heads."

Randy looks at Amy and gets a nod. "We'll be here at dawn and dispatch this bunch, one way or another."

The next morning, the duo was in the trading post having coffee with Ezra and Red Flower when five riders arrived. The gang entered, clearly liquored up, and demanded a case of whiskey. Ezra responded, "pay your outstanding balance of $61.48 and pay cash from now on or go elsewhere for your whiskey."

The lead outlaw, nodded to his Segundo, who pulled out a knife and was about to cut Red Flower. Randy saw that Red Flower was in serious trouble and drew his pistol. Without hesitating, he shot the outlaw in the foot. The outlaw collapsed to the floor and the remainder of the gang were going for their guns. Amy shot up from an isle with her cocked shotgun saying, "anyone pulling his gun out of the holster is a dead man."

The gang's leader said, "there's no woman that would shoot us with a shotgun. Take her down Chester"

Chester smiled as he pulled his pistol out and pointed it at Amy. That was his last move as Amy pulled the trigger and blasted him in the belly with a full load of buckshot. At the same time, Randy cocked his pistol and said, "any one else want to die?"

When hands went up, Ezra applied manacles to the four living outlaws. Randy then checked their pockets and collected $242. Amy went to check the outlaw's saddlebags and came back with $687. Ezra then loaded the dead outlaw on his horse's saddle and helped the groaning man with a hole in his foot onto his horse. With the remaining outlaws anchored with a neck collar chained to the stirrups, Randy went back in the trading post to settle with Ezra. He handed him $500 for his trouble and told him he would be back in two days after he delivered his prisoners to the law in Texas.

The duo pushed the horses to make the 25-mile ride back to Sheriff Craighead before dark. Resting and watering their horses every two hours, the outlaws wanted to get down and relieve themselves. Randy said, "I don't care about your wants and needs. You're nothing but animals going to market. Keep on complaining and you'll get a taste of a switch."

Amy knew he meant what he said and came back with a hardwood switch. The leader of the gang protested and swore at Randy. When he kept saying, "I'm going to kill you two someday," Amy had had enough and walked up to the boss-man and smacked him twice in the face with the switch.

The outlaw was furious and acted naturally by dismounting on the left. However, he forgot that his neck collar was chained to the right stirrup, and in the process nearly hung himself. Amy had no pity and started whipping him with the switch until he mounted back on his horse. Randy just smiled and thought, *now there is one woman I wouldn't get on her bad side*, and added, "does anyone want to cross my wife today?"

With no other confrontational takers, the caravan resumed its trek back to the Texas border town. They arrived in late afternoon and found Sheriff Craighead in his office talking to a man with a badge on his vest. Sheriff Craighead said, "I knew you would arrive with some outlaws, so I decided to hire a deputy to help as jailer. Meet Sandy Moore. It looks like we have four living customers, one dead and one with a bloody boot. Guess we'll need Doc's services."

After jailing them, the manacles and cervical collars were removed. The sheriff started matching faces with posters and finally said, "Well Mr. and Mrs. bounty hunters, you just captured the Bart gang. The leader, Ransom Bart has a $2,000 bounty for murder in three states. The four gang members will pay a total of $3,000. A total of $5,000 minus my 10%=$500 plus $20 for the undertaker."

Looking at the deputy, Amy asked, "do you have a pistol, rifle and horse?"

"No ma'am."

Amy goes to the horses and comes back with a Colt 44-40, a Win 73 rifle in the same caliber, a saddlebag full of 44-40 ammo and tells the deputy to go to the railing and select an outlaw horse to his liking.

Amy asks the sheriff, "do you need anything?"

"No, but thanks for gearing up my deputy. I'll process the rewards and I'll deposit the vouchers into your new joint account."

Before leaving town, the duo led the outlaw saddled horses to the town livery. Rusty Creymore was the hostler and a shrewd one to boot. Randy dickered and finally ended up with $240 for the four saddled horses. The price was a bit low, but Randy knew he would be dealing with this same man in the future.

Going to the town mercantile, Waldo Penderson, was interested in buying the four pistols and rifles. He paid $20 for the pistols and $30 for the rifles. Their last stop was the local bank. There they deposited the extra cash they accumulated from the outlaw horses, guns and petty cash.

Since it was late in the day, the duo had a nice home cooked chicken pie dinner at Sil's Diner. They then took a room in the Samson Hotel to get a good night sleep in a real bed and use the water closet/tub. While the hot water was being drawn, Amy stood there in her birthday suit and said, "you decided to stay overnight in the hotel so you could see me naked, heh?"

"Of course, and it was worth the entire $2 expense for the visual pleasure. Now get washed so we can enjoy other parts, and not just our eyes."

"Maybe we can convince Ezra to build a hotel at the trading post, that way we could hunt outlaws in style, heh?"

"Sounds like you already forgot our initial agreement—there are no luxuries on the bounty hunting trail."

After the bath, the remainder of the night was filled with much activity and very little sleep.

The next morning, after a replenishing breakfast, the duo headed back to the Indian Nations. Stopping by the trading post, Ezra was in a tizzy. There was an outlaw camp that was short of money and had robbed him of $192. To make it worse, this gang was also robbing other outlaw camps, forcing me to extend credit. Do you think you can help me out?"

"Of course, but you have to keep in mind that bringing two outlaw camps in a row may alert the other camps against you and in turn will hurt your business. That's why we were thinking of heading to the Indian encampments to look for outlaws."

"I agree, but this Lynch gang is killing my business. If you could arrest this gang, then head to the Cheyenne tribe. This tribe is more receptive to bounty hunters. Because of their leader, Chief Blue Sky, they will help you find outlaws hiding in other Cheyenne camps."

Amy could see the advantage in helping Ezra out, so when Randy looked at her for a sign, she quickly nodded yes. Randy explained to Ezra how they would proceed. "I strongly believe that if we go and attack their camp that we'll have to kill most of them. That's not how we operate. We would rather let the quarry come to us in piecemeal fashion. These outlaws will be sending one of their gang to pickup whiskey and supplies and we'll be here waiting for him."

The next day, as expected, Ezra recognized a customer as one of the gang in question. With a signal to the duo, Amy stepped up to him, with her shirt partially unbuttoned, to get his attention as Randy stepped behind him and dropped his pistol barrel on his head. The outlaw was manacled and moved to the wood shed with a neck collar tied to the shed's frame. With his mouth gagged and Rocky sitting by, the man was totally out of commission.

The next day, with his man missing, Lynch sent two of his men to find out what happened to the first man. When these two arrived, both were captured and imprisoned in shackles and gagged. Now Rocky had three specimens to guard.

The third day, the entire Lynch gang was now expected to arrive at the trading post, and not in a very good mood. Randy tried to send Ezra and Red Flower to go visit Red Flower's family, but they refused. Both said they wanted to protect their life's work and help the duo. So, Randy set up a scenario. Red Flower would hide next to the front porch and when the shooting started, she was to arrest the man holding the reins and shoot him if he resisted or drew on her. Ezra was to work the counter as usual with his pistol at his side. The duo was walking the tables of food and other supplies, acting as normal customers but with their backpacks and loaded shotguns. This time Amy had Rocky at her side to intimidate the outlaws.

To everyone's surprise, eight men arrived at a full gallop. With one man staying with the horses, the other seven entered and spread out all over the post. There were seven separated targets which made for a real dangerous mess. As expected, all seven men had their pistols drawn as they entered. Lynch was the only one to speak as he started, "I'm going to only ask you once, where are my three men I sent here to get supplies?"

There was no time to answer, Randy pulled his sawed-off shotgun out and shot two outlaws dead. Amy shouted, "there are two more buckshot loads in my shotgun for anyone moving. At the same time, Rocky was ordered to attack, and took a large bite of Lynch's calf and started to drag him about. At the same time, Ezra had drawn his pistol, and seeing an outlaw ready to shoot Rocky, pulled the trigger and shot the outlaw in the face. While this is all happening, Randy is busy reloading his shotgun as they heard a shotgun blast outside, and all knew that Red Flower had done her job.

At the end of the gunfight, the trading post was full of acrid smoke with very little visibility. Eventually a tally revealed four dead outlaws, three already hog tied in the wood shed, one injured with a deep dog bite, and three other outlaws with their hands up—for a total of eleven men finally taken out of the outlaw ranks.

Amy could not believe that they had seven live outlaws to bring back to Texas with only four neck collars to secure them to the stirrups. Randy went thru the wanted posters as Ezra was loading the outlaws onto their horses, dead or alive. Wanted posters were available for all of eight outlaws. Three younger outlaws, who had put their hands up, had no bounties. When he segregated these three, he got this story:

"We are sons of poor homesteaders who were recruited by Lynch to rob outlaws. We never knew he planned to rob Mr. McCullock. We have not killed anyone and haven't even received any money from robbing the outlaws. We made a bad choice for once in our lives and for that we're in real trouble."

"I see, well I believe that everyone should be offered a second chance after one big mistake. If you are willing to return to your homesteads and not get on the owlhoot trail again, I'm willing to let you go if it's ok with Amy, Ezra and Red Flower."

All three young men thanked Randy as they waited for the other's vote. One by one, they all agreed to let them leave to go back to Texas. Now things were better balanced with four live outlaws to be fitted to the neck collars and four dead ones tied to their horse's saddle.

During one of the rest stops, Amy was watching the outlaws from afar. Randy was busy tightening cinches and never saw one of the manacled outlaws sliding a derringer out of his vest pocket. He was about to point it at Randy when a pistol shot ran out and the outlaw collapsed to the ground while dropping the derringer. Amy went up to the outlaw and said, "you're lucky I only shot you in the arm, now you'll hang for sure, which is your comeuppance for sure."

The duo and Rocky pushed hard to get to Sheriff Craighead before dark. Arriving, Deputy Sandy Moore was in the office. The sheriff came out of the privy and greeted the duo. "Well, looks like we have another batch, heh!"

"Yes, this is the Lynch gang and all eight can be identified by their wanted posters."

"Let's cut to the chase, what is the total bounty on this gang?"

Amy chimes in, "looks to us as $6,000."

"Ok, that's $500 to me and $100 to Sandy. And $60 for the undertaker."

"Sounds good to us. Now how did you get rid of the last gang we brought you?"

"When I notified Wells Fargo, who posted the rewards, they insisted in sending a jail wagon with guards to bring the gang alive to Amarillo for trial. I suspect that the same will happen with this batch."

"How long will it take to get the telegraph vouchers on these?"

"A couple of days."

"This time, we'll wait for the vouchers so we can do our banking before returning to the Indian Nations."

For the next days, they bathed, and Randy got a shave and haircut. They got all their clothes laundered, spent some time in the local saloon playing poker and of course their evenings in their hotel room.

Amy pointed something to Randy, "during the day you treat me as a business partner. Once we enter our hotel room or get into our tent, you revert to your second personality—romantic, lustful and loving."

"That's true, our bedroom is our private haven where we pleasure ourselves and make love. What happens in the tent or hotel room is between us and never to be divulged."

"Yes, what we do should never be divulged for fear of being given forty lashes by the jealous brigade."

Once the reward vouchers came in, the duo brought their funds to their joint bank account. Issued a bank draft for the sheriff, deputy and undertaker. The petty cash totaling $897 from the outlaw's pockets and saddlebags was deposited except for $200 in petty working cash. The sale of eight saddled horses to Rusty Creymore's livery totaled $480 and the sale of eight pistols and rifles to Waldo Emerson's Mercantile came to another $400.

Walking out of the bank, Amy asked, "are we planning on bounty hunting for the year, or do we quit when we have an adequate nest egg?"

"Neither, we quit when our reputation becomes a hindrance to us continuing bounty hunting safely. Eventually, our reputation as successful hunters will turn on us, and the outlaws will be hunting us as a threat to them and their friends."

***

Returning to the Nations, the duo went straight to the trading post. Ezra confirmed that it was time for the camping outlaws to be given a reprieve from the duo. There was talk that they were coming to hunt for them if they returned to the area.

Ezra said, "ride north some ten miles to Well's Stream. This stream is at least ten feet wide, easily recognizable, and runs northeast to the Cheyenne Nation some five miles away. Look up Chief Blue Sky and good luck."

The duo had no trouble following Ezra's directions and before they realized it, were on a butte looking down at an Indian encampment with hundreds of tepees. Amy had reservations to head closer and asked, "are you sure we are safe, I don't trust Indians especially when there are two of us with a dog compared to hundreds of warriors."

"Trust me dear, I know what I'm doing!"

Amy thought?" *Yeah, like I trust your every night, but I missed my monthly a week ago— trusting you.*

Approaching the camp, a young warrior came galloping towards them and stopped in their faces holding a war spear and saying, "why you come here?"

Randy slowly reached in his saddlebags, pulled out a neck collar with chain and his deputy badge. He handed the items to the Indian and added, "Chief Blue Sky."

The Indian took both items and said, "follow."

Riding thru camp, they were gawked at but never touched. Several dogs snarled at Rocky who growled back and sent the other dogs running with their tail between their legs. When they arrived at an unusually large and unique teepee, the warrior signed us to dismount and wait. During the waiting, the duo was surrounded by a half dozen stoic warriors. Suddenly the teepee's flap opened, and a well adorned elderly Indian came out holding the sheriff's badge and the neck collar. The Indian Chief spoke, "you know 'Wane and Kal?'"

"I know of them; they are now well known in our country. My wife and I are bounty hunters like them."

"Wife a hunter? Ugg. Wife is squaw to serve warrior!" Stay, we talk after we eat. Squaw will put up new teepee for you."

The chief walks back into his teepee after he spoke to the warriors and squaws in his native tongue. The warriors backed off and the squaws started erecting a new teepee while others were preparing a feast on the fires. The duo's four horses were walked to the corral, as they kept their saddles, guns, saddlebags and panniers. In incredible time, a new teepee was set up and a small fire started inside. The teepee's floor was covered with hides and several blankets were added to make sitting benches. The duo placed their belongings in one corner and kept the remaining spaces for sitting and sleeping.

When the feast was ready, the duo was escorted next to the Chief. Amy especially liked the Pemmican made from beef, fat, corn, molasses and several other ingredients. Randy liked the pan-fried venison liver— or what he thought was liver or even venison. Mixed with their native breads, it was a good meal. To the duo's surprise they were offered real coffee after the meal with a dessert made with dried apples.

The Chief started talking while smoking a cheroot. "You know, we get many foods from Ezra's Trading Post. We trade our pelts for food, cheroots, coffee, blankets and live cattle. My tribe does not trade for whiskey. Other groups of Cheyenne prefer to house outlaws instead of trapping for pelts. Each outlaw pays $40 per moon cycle for a three man teepee and two food servings per day."

The duo was listening intently when the Chief shocked them. "I tell you where outlaws are, you capture outlaws, and give Indians one out of twenty parts of bounty. Yes?"

"For a 5% share, you have a deal, Chief."

"This word deal, is good, yes?"

"Oh, yes."

The Chief throws away his cheroot and says, "we smoke peace pipe with real Texas tobacco and make the 'deal.'"

***

After the peace pipe, Randy explained to Chief Blue Sky, "it would be impossible to go into an Indian camp and arrest these outlaws.

These men are guaranteed sanctuary and so the Indians are not going to let their 'charges' go without a fight." The Chief agreed and asked how this could be done.

"Where are these outlaw's teepees?"

"On the edge of the camp, away from the Indian families."

"Great. In the middle of the night, when the outlaws are in a drunken sleep, can your warriors sneak in the teepees and steal their whiskey. That will force them to come to the trading post to get more whiskey. Amy and I will be waiting for them and capture them. The Indians will assume that they left for good and won't come looking for them."

"Done, my warriors will do this. Plus, we will sell the whiskey to Ezra for cattle. That is also a good 'deal.' This will rid the tribe of Maggot and his five killers."

"Maggot? You mean the Magoon gang." Looking at the wanted posters, Randy adds up the bounties that totaled $8,200 for all six men. Before leaving, Amy hands Chief Blue Sky a bag of $20 double eagle gold pieces for $420 which was a bit over his 5% share of the bounty.

Several days later, an Indian messenger came to the duo's camp. The message was that the outlaws were without whiskey. The duo closed camp and went to the trading post before the gang arrived. This time, the duo convinced Ezra and Red Flower that this was not their fight and convinced them to leave for the day. Randy took over the counter and Amy was unloading supplies when the gang arrived.

Without any warning, all six violent men

entered the trading post. Magoon came up to Randy and said, "where is Ezra"

"Went to Texas to order more supplies, I'm his fill in."

"We were robbed last night of twelve bottles of whiskey. Has any Indians come in to trade them for supplies."

"I've been here since dawn, and you're the first customers."

"Crap! I want twelve bottles on credit."

"Randy pulls out twelve bottles to keep the gang off balance. Suddenly Amy draws her Colt and yells out, "put your hands up, we're taking you back to Texas for your bounty, dead or alive."

Magoon realized that they were being called out as he and his toadies all pulled their pistols. The trading post became a madhouse of shooting and gun smoke. When the shooting ended, Magoon stood bleeding from a gunshot to the right shoulder, another had a bad wound to his left hip, two lay dead on the floor, and two had their hands in the air. Randy got hit in his side below the belt, but the bullet went thru and did not enter his belly.

The first thing they did was to manacle the four living outlaws. Amy cleaned Randy's wound, applied carbolic acid to prevent infection, and bandaged the area. Randy started to pull his britches up as Amy added, "there's no rush to pull up your britches, I'm enjoying the view. Things are much clearer and bigger in daylight, heh!"

With four neck collars applied, secured to a stirrup, and the two dead outlaws tied to their saddles, the caravan headed out to the border town and Sheriff Craighead.

Delivering his prisoners, their identity was quickly confirmed by Sheriff Craighead. While writing out a bank voucher to the sheriff and his deputy, a telegrapher arrived on a dead run. "Mr. McWain, this gram just arrived from Wichita Falls. It's labeled, emergency and delivery requested."

"Amy grabbed the telegram and read:

From: Marshall Omer McDonald--stop

To: Randy and Amy McWain--stop
Multiple kidnappings—stop
Texas rangers not available—stop
Need to infiltrate human trafficking group—stop
Need immediate assistance—stop
Awaiting response—stop

Amy looked at Randy for his nod. When she got it, she tells the telegrapher, "here is a dollar, send this response—leaving now and will arrive in 48 hours."

Randy gave instructions to the sheriff, paid his 10% and asked him to sell the outlaw horses, guns and saddlebag contents. The cash from the outlaw pockets came up to $700, of which the duo kept $200 for expenses. Sheriff Craihead agreed to deposit all the funds into their bank accounts.

After replenishing their food supplies, the duo was on a dead run to Amarillo some 100 miles away. There they would take the train to Wichita Falls to enter into a completely different hunt. Randy surmised that Amy would play a major role in this caper but had mixed feelings about it. However, first they needed to get there and talk it over with Marshall McDonald.

***

CHAPTER 10

FINAL CAPER

The duo was pushing hard all day. The horses had been well rested and fed so were able to handle the demands of their riders. Rocky had to hop on the packhorse's saddle about half the time. Despite resting and watering the horses every two hours, Amy was totally exhausted by the time darkness arrived and they made camp.

While Randy started dinner, Amy had to go to the bushes with her saddlebags. When she returned next to Randy she said, "Pounding so hard on the saddle today started my late monthly. Guess I'm not pregnant after all."

"Are you happy or sad?"

"Both, but knowing what caper likely lies ahead, it's probably best this way."

During the night, Amy had to make hygienic changes several times. Seeing her needs, Randy made it clear to Amy that if she needed to stop before the two-hour rest period to say so. After a full breakfast for all, the duo was back on the trail.

As they approached Amarillo, the duo traveled thru some desert like area with black muck on the ground. Randy stopped to check this stuff out and said, "this is that lubricating stuff called oil. There is a lot of seepage in this area. Do you know who owns this land?"

"No, but we are approaching a house ahead, let's stop to enquire. The lady who greeted them gave the duo's their names, Ed and Samantha Craymore. They were retired and did not own any of the land that was open range for sale by the property office in Amarillo. Randy placed the information aside for future use.

Arriving at the railroad yard as darkness was setting, the duo was in luck. There was a overnight express to Wichita Falls leaving in one hour. After buying two tickets and getting the tags for the four horses and Rocky, the duo headed to the nearby diner for a full meal of prime roast beef with baked potatoes and gravy.

The train had only one passenger car, one stock car and four open cars of coal for home use. On schedule, the train departed. Being mesmerized by the clanging sound of connecting rails and dimmed lamps, the exhausted duo fell asleep. They woke up when the train stopped at a coaling station. The fireman would open the side chute and refill the forward sloped tender with coal as another worker filled the water tank from the water silo. Despite being in the middle of the night, there were frequently passengers to board the train.

After being on horses for the past month, it was a luxury to be traveling at 20—40 mph. With the heavy coal cars requiring frequent stops at coaling/water stations, the conductor said they were making 25 mph. That meant they would travel the 200 miles to Wichita Falls in eight hours and would arrive at the crack of dawn.

Arriving a bit late, the duo brought the four horses and Rocky to the nearest livery and made indefinite arrangements with a deposit of $10. Their next stop was Marshall McDonald's office. To their surprise, Sheriff Samuels was also present as well as two new deputies.

"Thank you all for being here this morning, how did you know we'd be on this specific coal train?"

"Pretty easy with the telegraph. So, let me tell you the problem. We have had ten women kidnapped in the past two weeks. We are assuming that a human trafficking ring from Houston is to blame. Since they kidnapped the Judge's wife last night, we don't think the ladies have been moved yet."

With the train the only way out of town, I suspect that is not the game plan since we can control who leaves town by train. But go on."

"What we need is for a woman to go undercover. We need to know where the gals are being kept and we need to know who the leaders and organizers are, so we can arrest them. The undercover gal needs to be a professional. If necessary, she needs to be aggressive, seductive and proficient with a weapon to dispatch the guards. That means you Amy. We desperately need you. What say you?"

"Wait a minute now, this is a very dangerous assignment. What protection can you provide Amy and what are the financial rewards?"

"If we are called in, the four of us will be there to assist you. As far as financial rewards, these men may be wanted outlaws but there is no guarantee. Judge Eckert is presently meeting with the parents, husbands and lovers of the kidnapped gals. These are well to do business men in town, and I expect you'll be called to the courthouse anytime, and here is a court messenger with a message for you."

Randy reads the note, and says, "you were right, where is the courthouse?'

"Just follow the messenger."

The meeting was held in the courtroom area. Judge Eckert was sitting at the prosecutor's table and ten men surrounded them.

Judge Eckert started. "Thank you for coming. Your reputation dealing with criminals is well established. You have sand and get results. We all believe that our loved ones have been taken for ransom. Yesterday, the hardware owner got a note saying, if he paid a generous ransom, his wife would be returned unharmed. It also included the fact that a payment of $5,000 would not be acceptable and he would receive one of his wife's fingers instead of his returning wife. A second low payment would get him one of his wife's nipples in return."

"It certainly sounds like these evil men have the advantage and are calling the shots. What are you offering for compensation if we return the ladies unharmed."

"$5,000 for each unharmed gal to a maximum of $50,000 in US currency. Any dead or captured outlaw's rewards are yours, including their guns, horses, saddles and saddlebag belongings. Any confiscated property, such as land or buildings, reverts back to the town."

"Fair enough, Amy and I need to talk, we'll step out for a few minutes. Please wait here."

Amy took the lead, "I can do this, and I want it."

"Keep in mind, being kidnapped will put you at a disadvantage."

"Randy, this is the nest egg we were talking about. If we do this caper, we can retire and change our lives. For the whole year, you have taken the lead and taken more risks than me. Now it's time for me to step up and do my part."

"It's hard to counter point your argument when I know you're right from a business sense. But you're the love of my life and I cannot lose you no matter what the rewards."

"You're not getting rid of me. Now start thinking how we can hide some weapon in my clothes or body parts."

Returning to the courtroom, "Ok, gentlemen, you have a deal. If everything goes to plan, Amy will be kidnapped tonight, and the rescue process will start tomorrow."

"Amy, go to the mercantile and get a revealing dress. The kind that hangs over the shoulders and reveals a large amount of skin. Let the bosoms fall naturally without bindings. Make sure the dress reaches just above the ground. For hair decorations, get some flowered bases with three-inch pins. Lastly, get a bottle of potent ladies' perfume. While you're shopping, I will make you some weapons we can hide on you."

When Amy returned, Randy was just finished making two weapons. "These are narrow knives called Arkansas picks."

"How can you secure that inside my body parts?"

"No silly, we can't put anything inside of you. If they have any brains, they'll do a cavity search when you are thrown in with the other victims. We're going to sew the blades in the hem of your dress."

"Cavity search, heh! There's no doubt now, those guards are going down."

The duo went to get dinner at the Hotel restaurant and then Amy got gussied up again. Wearing that lavender perfume was overpowering. Randy takes the dress's hem and pours the perfume on it and then takes a rag and pours the rest of the perfume over it. Presenting the rag to Rocky, he stepped back sneezing, but Randy knew he had a smell that would stay with him.

"Ok, we're ready. Now I expect that when you go to the privy, you'll be kidnapped and brought on horseback to their hideout. The perfume scent on your dress will keep Rocky on your trail. Remember, I'll always be outside the place you are held. A loud call and I'll be there in seconds. Once you're in, it's up to you to devise a rescue."

"Let's go, and I plan to make you proud of me."

***

Walking in the Crazy Eight Casino and Saloon, neither of the duo were wearing their rings. Randy was dressed in a three-piece grey suit with a 10-gallon white Texas hat and a Texas shoelace necktie. Amy looked like a trophy doll. The couple overflowed with the appearance of excessive wealth. What the duo did not know was that the Casino owner, Mel Shuster, had noticed the couple and had instructed one of his toadies to set up for the abduction.

The duo was spending money at the roulette table and Randy gave the impression of drinking heavily. Amy excused herself and headed to the outside privy. Coming out she was abducted by two men at gun point, gagged and tied to the saddle horn. Her horse was led down the back streets to parts unknown.

Meanwhile, Randy managed to act very drunk and rowdy. The bouncers came over and invited him to leave. Glad to cooperate, Randy ran to the livery to get his horse and Rocky. Bringing Rocky to the privy where Amy disappeared, Randy presented the scented rag, and Rocky took off with his nose to the ground.

Meanwhile, Amy had traveled blindfolded till they reached an old abandoned homestead. Being guided to a small office, she was instructed by a female voice to drop her dress and her underwear. Keeping the blindfold on, she was ordered to turn around and bend over. Amy was totally mortified when both her cavities were roughly explored. When done, the attacker checked Amy's dress and underwear. When satisfied, she told Amy to redress and join the other women where the male guards would remove her blindfold.

Meanwhile on the road, a mile away, Rocky stops beside an access road and looks at Randy. Randy steps down and walks his horse behind Rocky. After a sharp bend, Rocky stopped and sat on his haunches. Out some 200 yards was an old house and barn. The lights were on inside the barn and two men stood outside standing guard with shotguns at port-arms. Randy walked inside the trees and stopped 50 yards from the front door and waited.

Back inside, Amy met with most of the ladies and was satisfied to find three ladies who were willing to shoot their way out of the barn once she dispatched the two-armed guards hovering over the ladies. She also found out that everyone was being held for ransom and not for transporting to large cities into prostitution. Later that night when the ladies were sleeping, Amy decided that the sooner she dispatched these two guards, the sooner they could all get out—besides she knew Randy was outside and would be available if she called him.

Amy seductively walked up to one of the guards who was awake. She said, "I see your partner is sleeping, that puts all the responsibility on your shoulders. Maybe you'd like some company or whatever?"

"What 'whatever' do you have in mind sweetie."

To not lose this piss-ant's attention, she pulls her dress off her right shoulder and bares her right breast. The guard's eyebrows pulled up and his mouth fell open. "Heck, I can get that in any whore house."

"True, but it comes with a bonus. I'm a wealthy gal and will include $10,000 in your pocket if you let me escape out the back door. To guarantee the deal, you can have some of this now." Amy pulls her dress up, still holding the hem, and starts pulling her underpants down. To better see, the guard bends down as Amy pulls the Arkansas pick from the dress's hem and shoves it deep inside the guard's ear.

The guard stiffened, stood erect and made a guttural sound before he collapsed to the floor in a major convulsion. Amy quickly reacted, pulled her dress over her shoulder and yells out to the sleeping guard. As he comes over to see his friend thrashing about the floor, he asks, "what happened to him?"

"I don't know, he called out that he needed help and just collapsed into these shaking gyrations." The guard spots blood coming out of his partner's ear and bends over to get a better look. Suddenly, he saw the blade and was about to turn to look at Amy when she reacted. Quickly, she takes one of her hair pins and shoves the three-inch pin into the guards eye. The guard's scream was so loud that all the women awoke. Amy stopped the screaming by hitting the hair pin with her fist and shoved the pin into the guard's brain. Before all to see, both guards were on the floor in uncontrolled convulsions till the last throws of life ended their misery.

Amy starts pulling pistols and rifles and hands them to the three ladies. "Get ready, the outside guards will be rushing in. I'll handle the first two, then I'll need your help with the others. As expected, the door opened and the first guard was shot in the face by Amy, the second guard knew he was doomed, so he put his hands up and said, "I give up, don't shoot."

Amy nonchalantly steps outside and yells out, "hey Randy, come out. We have a live one who needs your awl."

Randy rushed in and grabbed Amy in a crushing embrace. "I must have been insane to let you do this, when one guard screamed out, I nearly wet myself because I couldn't do anything to help you. Never, Never, Never again. Do you hear? "Yes dear, I love you too. Now make this guard sing so we can get the head of this fiasco as well as that woman who grossed me out."

While the ladies were making breakfast, Randy took the guard outside to talk with him. "Listen here, I can make you talk, so you can save yourself some unbearable pain. Plus, if you tell me what I want to know, I'll convince the judge to give you a light prison sentence instead of hanging you for kidnapping."

"My name is George Bisley. I want to live and want out of the outlaw life. The man in charge is Mel Shuster, the owner of the Crazy Eight Casino. His wife Valerie checked out the gals, and his saloon manager, Daryl Rickert, is the man who brought the girls here."

"Thanks, and you have my word, I'll speak to the judge on your behalf."

Later that day, a huge wagon arrived at the courthouse with all the hostages, alive and well. Three dead men went to the undertaker after they were identified by George. Marshal McDonald confirmed the dead men's identity and would check if they were wanted men.

While the reunion was in progress, the judge came to the duo and thanked them for saving his wife. Along with the thanks, the judge handed the duo bank drafts totaling $50,000. Randy added, "and Amy and I are heading to get the ring leaders, free of charge, heh."

Arriving at the Crazy Eight, the duo headed for the owner's office. On the way thru the Casino, Amy kicks a chair and breaks off a leg which she brings along. Busting thru the office, Mel and Valerie were standing by the desk talking. Without warning, Amy swings the chair leg and smashes it into Valerie's face, knocking her to the ground with several teeth blowing out of her mouth. Amy screams, I should have put that wooden stick up your cavities, but it was too smooth. I really wanted a rough 2X4 up your cavities, but the busted mouth will mark you for life." During this attack, Daryl tried to stand up as Randy smacked him in the head with the butt of his pistol. Mel tried to object when Rocky was ordered to attack as he grabbed Mel's chin and bit down, with an unbelievable shocked appearance on Shuster's face.

When ordered down, Mel was grabbing his chin in horror. Randy then spoke up, "now I know you're not smart enough to be the kidnapping organizer. Someone was telling you who to kidnap and you had the perfect location to make it happen—just like my wife was kidnapped from the outside privy. Now kidnapping is a hanging offense and the judge is not in a good mood since you kidnapped his wife. If I were you, I'd spill the beans who your partner is."

"Go to hell."

"Suit yourself." Randy throws Mel to the

floor, opens his mouth and shoves the awl in a bad tooth, pulls it out and shoves it into another bad molar. This time he left the awl in place and started giggling it around. Mel was beside himself and started to mumble something that sounded like 'enough." Randy backed off and Mel spoke.

"A financier by the name of Gilmore Harps. He managed the finances and investments of the family members. That's how we knew who had the cash to pay the ransoms. You'll find him in his office on the corner of Main and Autumn Street."

Marshall McDonald was waiting outside and agreed to bring all three to jail. The duo headed to Harp's office. Arriving, they busted the entrance door and Randy jumped on Harp's desk, grabbed him by the collar, and punched him in the face a half dozen times. The glasses were shattered, his nose flattened, and one eye socket blown out. "Now, that's only part of your comeuppance, you'll hang as well for your miserly need for money and disregard for humanity. Now get on your feet, you're going to jail. For an educated man, you're certainly one stupid sumbitch. Fortunately, the hangman's rope is the ultimate cure for stupidity—since we all know we can't fix stupid!"

Amy exclaimed, "It would have been easier on your knuckles if you had used my second Arkansas pick, heh."

"Well, being the end of our bounty hunting year, pummeling him was more rewarding, heh."

Several days later, the trial was held. Valerie was sentenced to 20 years in prison. George Bisley was sentenced to 10 years and Mel Shuster got life in prison. Gilmore Harps was sentenced to hang. The court confiscated the Crazy Eight Saloon and Harps office building and returned the real-state to the town. The duo was allowed possession of seven saddled horses, five rifles and pistols and $398 in petty cash.

The next morning, after the hanging, the duo sold the horses for $490 and the firearms for $265. Marshall McDonald was paid $150 for the use of his jail. To the duos' surprise, the total bounty rewards came to $6,500 for dead or alive outlaws. Then, they decided to stay in town for a few days, to open a bank account and to plan their future.

What neither of them realized was that a new page in their lives was just about to begin. Amy from an experience before the bounty year, and for Randy from an exposure during his recent traveling thru Texas.

***

BOOK FOUR

MCWAIN ENTERPRISES

CHAPTER 11

CHANGING TIMES

Randy and Amy decided to spend some time in the luxury and comfort of the hotel and the many diners. There were several mercantiles for Amy to shop for dresses. Randy realized how gorgeous his wife was in a dress and asked that she abandon the shirt, britches and gunbelt. For personal protection, Randy gave Amy a Remington derringer in 41 caliber to hide in her pockets, and a new Webley Bulldog 44 for her reticule.

One day, while Amy was trying on some dresses, Randy was visiting the store's book department. He found two listed books that covered two potential business opportunities. With a certain extra fee, these books could be ordered by telegraph and would be arriving as early as noon tomorrow by train. Without mentioning it to Amy, he ordered the two books and paid the special delivery fee.

The next day after a late replenishing lunch, the subject of their future came up. Randy started, "out of curiosity, is there any profession or business enterprise that you might be interested in pursuing."

"Before our time on the hunt, I was a competent gunsmith and leather worker. The part I enjoyed the most was making gun holsters. Other than the cutting and sewing, was the tooling and engraving. It allowed me to use my creative skills. If I had a choice, I would like to make holsters for a living, but I know that's a tight niche to survive in a Texas town. What do you think?"

"I have some great ideas on the matter. To get started, I have a two-book package waiting at the railroad yard. Yours is a book on how to start, maintain and grow a business. I suspect that leather products would fit right in as a starter business. Read the book and we'll talk again. I'm eager to see if the book's ideas match my own."

"Wow, I see you've been planning ahead. Now, how about you. Is there a potential business you might be interested in?"

"Yes, there are two. The first is to help you make your dream come true. It will take both of us to make such a leather business profitable. The second is oil."

"Oil, that greasy stuff we found around Amarillo. How can you make money with that messy stuff?"

"That is the subject of the book I ordered for me. I suspect we'll have to read each other's book so we can discuss the two business options, heh?"

"Sounds great to me, let's go to the railroad depot to get our books so we can start reading."

The afternoon was spent reading at different locations. Their hotel room, the hotel lobby and restaurant, their favorite diner, a park bench and chairs on the hotel porch. The books were large texts and by dinner time they had gone thru half the pages. After a quick dinner, both hooked readers were sitting in their nightdress reading.

Randy suggested that they could put their books down for some pleasurable time. "Now that I don't have to be careful, things could be much more interesting."

"Not now, I'm in a good part of the book—money. We can't lose daylight to read. On second thought, a careless quickie may be in order, plus, we can always read by lamp light."

The quickie turned into a marathon and an hour later, the duo was sitting at the room's table with a coal lamp between their books. By morning, Randy arranged to have room service bring them a large pot of coffee and egg sandwiches. By noon, the duo finished their books and then exchanged them and continued reading. Dinner was sent up to the room. Chicken pot pie, bread pudding and plenty of coffee. They read into the late hours. To avoid losing an hour of reading time, both decided to skip a quickie that would turn into a marathon.

The next morning, another breakfast in the

room, skipping lunch and finally by dinner time both of them had read both books. They decided to have dinner in the hotel restaurant since it stayed open till 10PM nightly. Both Randy and Amy had so much to talk about, so they took an isolated table for their meal and discussion.

Randy started, "you have a product that will take you to a national level. Starting in Texas, the Cowboy will always be using a Colt Peacemaker and will need a selection of functional holsters. Now the eastern part of the country is wild about the Cowboy Way thanks to Buffalo Bill Cody's Wild West show that he has brought east and even into Europe. You have a product we can sell to all the gun shops in Texas and then spread throughout the West and Eastern USA. You make the holsters, and I'll find a market to sell them."

"I came into this discussion feeling that I had the drive to make a business, and only find that you have more than I do."

"I have big ideas and we'll go into this in a big way. Remember the one quote in the book, "you can't become wealthy selling your body by the hour. You need to hire people to work for you and let them make money for you. That's how you grow and become wealthy."

"I have one question; in what town do we build our new business?"

"Along the railroad line between Houston to Amarillo. The train and telegraph are crucial for a successful business—for orders, quick mail delivery, and shipping. With your parents in Amarillo and my mom two hours away by train in Childress, the answer to me is Amarillo. Besides my other interest also brings me to North Texas."

"Well, let's talk a bit about oil, before we go into the business specifics of making holsters."

"Ok. That black muck in the open range behind the Craymore home in Amarillo. That surface seepage often means the land is sitting on top of a crude oil reservoir or lake. Oil is the future of this country. Right now, it's used to lubricate machinery and fire private water boilers. In the near future, the trains will convert from coal fired boilers to oil for steam. Next to follow is refining it to make kerosene and replace coal oil lamps. A byproduct to distilling crude oil is gasoline. With internal combustion engine in the horizon, automobiles will follow which will run on gasoline. Eventually diesel engines will power large ships. It's even predicted that refined crude oil will be used to heat our homes. In short, an energy revolution is in the horizon and I want to be part of it."

"How do you plan to prepare for this speculation?"

"By buying land that has surface seepage."

"For now, it's time to acquire land with mineral rights that has potential and is somewhat accessible from Amarillo. In time, I will be building a derrick to dig our first well."

"So first, we buy land worth speculating. Then what?"

"I want approximately 30 sections of land with complete mineral rights."

"Ok, well a section of land is 640 acres. So, you want some 19,000 acres of land—all speculative. That's going to cost us over $21,000 by the time you pay the taxes and mineral rights."

"You're close. By the time I add an oil well, better assume the price will be closer to $27,000."

"And an oil well is also speculative, heh."

"I know it's a lot of money, but we have it. Remember it takes money to make money. We'll have plenty left over to invest in your enterprise."

"I agree, I'm only kidding you. After reading your book, there's no doubt in my mind that you'll become a wealthy 'oil man' in due time. It's just a bit nerve racking to invest so much money on a belief that oil will become so important a commodity."

"So, let's pack and take the train tomorrow. We need to buy land."

***

Their first stop was the Childress station. After shocking his mother with a wife, he found out she was very lonely with Randy's dad being gone. Amy even suggested she was depressed. When confronted by Randy, his mom agreed that all her friends had passed away and their seemed nothing around her that kept her interests."

Randy stepped aside to talk to Amy. "How would you feel if we moved mom with us to Amarillo. We can find a small house close to us and get her involved with our lives."

"I can't think of a better solution. Yes, let's do it."

"Would you make her the offer; I think this should come from a woman."

Randy stayed outside on the porch as Amy went to make the offer to Mrs. McWain.

"Mrs. McWain. . . . . .

"Amy, please call me Stella!"

"Ok, Stella. How would you like to move to Amarillo with us?"

"Oh no dear. I've lived in this house all my life and could never leave here."

Amy leaned forward and started whispering. All of a sudden Mrs. McWain exclaimed, "in that case, yes I'll move to Amarillo."

Randy heard his mom and walked back in the house. "Start packing and I'll put the house for sale."

"Just go to the bank and see President Earle Johnson. He's been after me for months to buy this house for one of his sons. I'm sure he'll give me a good price."

"Ok, I'll go make the sale and arrange for you to stay in the house till we find something for you in Amarillo."

Back on the train, Randy asks, "what on earth did you say to mom to make her change her mind so quickly?"

"I offered her a choice job in my new business and an opportunity to help us raise our children—day to day instead of from afar."

Before leaving Childress, Amy sent a telegram saying they would arrive by dinner time. The train ride to Amarillo took three hours. Arriving at the railroad depot, Amy spotted her parents waiting on the platform. Amy rushed out to jump into her parents' arms. Tears were flowing out of control. Suzanne started, "we've been so worried about you being on the outlaw trail. Are you really home to stay?"

Romeo added, "we've been following your capers in the local papers. Your last one in

Wichita Falls made headline news all over Texas and you're building a superb reputation."

"Well dad, that reputation is why we need to quit bounty hunting before it's too late. Yes mom, I'm here to stay. Now I want to present to you the love of my life, my husband Randy McWain."

After introductions, arrangements were made to leave their horses and Rocky at the nearby livery close to the Boudreau home. The Boudreau had their two-seat buggy waiting and proceeded home. The Boudreau's home was a two story two-bedroom house with a porch, garden and small barn for the horse and buggy. After a great dinner of pork roast and vegetables, the McWains explained their plans of building an oil empire and starting a leather works industry for Cowboy holsters.

"First, Amy and I are going to ride and find land with surface oil seepage. Once we have found what we want, we'll then look for a large building to purchase to set up our factory."

Romeo adds, "we have a manufacturing row which houses several factories to include: small household furniture, clothing, tinsmith-in tin cans, and shoes. I happen to know there is an empty warehouse after a stagecoach factory closed its doors. That warehouse may be what you are looking for."

Suzanne added, "not to be pushy, but there is a large home available down the street from us—in what is considered the merchants' domiciles. For now, we would love it if you stayed with us till you settle down."

Amy says, "Ok, we'll stay with you for now while we look for land, a factory site, and a home."

***

At daybreak, the duo was already riding the open range behind the Craymore homestead. For hours they rode around and found four large areas covered with black greasy surface sludge. Convinced this was land worth buying, they went straight to the land office.

"Good morning, I'm Mo Hancock, land agent, tax collector and town clerk. What are you looking for."

"We would like to buy some open range land behind the Craymore home."

"Why would you want that, it is barren land where even grass has trouble growing. Even the ranchers don't want it."

"That's ok, how much an acre and how many acres are for sale?"

"There are 10 sections, or 6,400 acres, for sale at the cheap price of $1 an acre. It includes one mile of town road frontage."

"How much for mineral rights?"

"$100 per sections, or $1,000."

"We'll take all ten sections with mineral rights. Here's a bank voucher from the First National Bank in Wichita Falls for $7,400. What will our taxes be next year?"

"$275 due Jan 1."

After the paper work was done, a deed signed by Mr. Hancock was registered with the town of Amarillo. Amy then asks, "do you have other similar desert like pieces of land within five miles of town."

"Yes, we have one on the east, and the other on the west of town. They are both nine sections of land and each has a mile of town road frontage. Mineral rights are the same price of $100 per section."

Randy adds, "we'll go check these two plots out and will be back before you close at what time?"

"I close at 6PM."

With detailed instructions and maps, the two areas were easily found. Several large puddles of crude oil were found at several locations and sludge seemed to be everywhere. The duo never hesitated to return to the land office and actually made it back by 4PM.

"Welcome back, is that the land you're interested in?"

"Yes, and we'll buy both lots with mineral rights."

"I need to tell you that I sent a telegram to the bank in Wichita Falls and they confirmed that your bank drafts are good up to $57,000. So, I guess we're ready to finalize these transactions. I can also tell you that you're doing the right thing. This land will yield a fortune in oil if you're willing to wait out the current lagging in 'supply and demand.'"

With double the paper work and time to register, the duo purchased another 18 sections of land for $11,520 plus $1,800 for mineral rights. The taxes would be $246 per each plot due also on Jan 1.

Amy adds them all up; $7,400+$11,520+$1,800=$20,720. The duo was back at the Boudreau by dinner time with three deeds. A total of 28 sections of land with permanent surface and deep mineral rights, and town road frontage for easy access—equal to +-18,000 acres.

***

The next morning, Romeo had arranged for a bank representative to meet with the duo at warehouse row. Arriving in the Boudreau's buggy, a well-dressed gentleman was waiting for them at the front door of a very large building.

"Hello, I'm Aloysius Greathouse, president of the 1st National Bank. I'm also a life-long friend of President Stanley Cosby of the 1st

National Bank in Wichita Falls. I'm happy to say that your reputation precedes you as well as the line of credit you hold with our bank chain."

Amy adds, "Nice to meet you, but I hope our bank account does not increase the value of this real-estate."

"It certainly is not to your disadvantage. Since the railroad caused the stagecoach enterprise to go bankrupt, we were left holding the mortgage. That means that we are eager to sell it since it hasn't sold now for one year."

Randy had heard enough and said, "very good, please show us around."

As they entered the building, the duo was totally captivated. The massive interior had been gutted except for three coal heating stoves and a double water closet.

President Greathouse started. "This building is 50 feet wide by 200 feet long or 10,000 sq. ft. Because of the wide span, there are permanent beam/posts in the center of the entire building. As you can see it is solid construction. The outside is board and batten and the inside walls are single boards covering a six-inch wall space for insulation. The ceiling is 8 feet high and is also insulated with wool batting. Despite its size, it's fairly easy to heat with a low insulated ceiling. The floor, as you can see is concrete which comes at a premium. All the buildings in this row of factories use city sewage lines. In the back is a windmill well for your own water supply. The building is on four acres and in the back are three other buildings. There is a 15-horse barn with piped in water and a hay loft. The small building is a fully enclosed coal bin. There is also a separate storage shed that is 20 by 40 feet. And for the coup-de-gras, look at the ceiling lanterns—gas lanterns thru city lines."

Silence followed the president's presentation. It was Amy who asked, "Well Randy, does this meet our short- or long-term goals?"

"Depends on the total cost of a mortgage and property taxes. Well Mr. Greathouse, what is the price for this building, at what % interest for a business loan and what are the yearly taxes?"

"The property taxes are $671 per year. This year they would be prorated at closing. A business loan with 20% down would be 2%. The town's real estate assessment lists the property value at $15,000."

"What balance on the principal was the bank stiffed with after the bankruptcy?"

"Good question, "$10,000. We would accept $12,000 to compensate for lost interest over the past year and allow for a small profit."

"Amy looks at Randy and after she gets the nod says, "will you accept $11,000 in cash, plus we'll pay our prorated taxes and we'll even transfer the balance of our account in the Wichita Falls 1st National Bank to your bank?"

"Well Mr. and Mrs. McWain, you have a deal. Let's go to the bank and do the paperwork. In an hour, you'll be the owners of your own factory building. Afterwards, I'm told you wish to see the Hollis house, and I'll be happy to show it to you."

**

It was a short ride to the Hollis house. On arriving, the grounds were well landscaped.

President Greathouse started. "This is a four-bedroom house—three upstairs and the master bedroom downstairs. The downstairs has a parlor, kitchen, dining room, large double office and a small room next to the master bedroom that can serve as a nursery. The downstairs has a fireplace and two heating stoves. There are two water closets and bathtubs—downstairs and upstairs."

As they entered the house, they were greeted by Mr. and Mrs. Hollis. "Hello, excuse the packing boxes, but we are moving to Houston in two days. I need specialized surgery which can only be done in Houston, plus our daughter and family lives there. We have purchased a small furnished house close to our daughter. So, this house is all furnished as you can see, and it's priced to sell."

President Greathouse adds, "it has cold and hot water in the kitchen and both water closets. There is a coal fired boiler in the cellar along with a coal bin. This house also includes city water, sewer and gas lamps. The property taxes are $374 per year—also prorated at closing. The house sits on 6 acres, has a three-horse barn with a carriage house. It comes with the three horses and buggy and has a four-acre pasture for the horses to graze and exercise."

Mrs. Hollis joined the presentation. "As you can see, this house is completely furnished to include curtains, kitchen utensils and even the linen for all the beds. The only unfurnished room is the nursery."

Mrs. Hollis started the tour, room to room. Most of the questions came from Amy. During the tour, Randy made the comment. This is a real turn-key house that could last us a lifetime. The office already has two large desks, filing cabinets, gun cabinet, book-shelves and other office accessories."

After the tour, everyone sat at the dining table for negotiations. Randy started, "Well, Mr. and Mrs. Hollis, what are you asking for this magnificent house?"

"We are willing to let it go at a discount, since we would like our money before leaving town in two days."

Amy adds, "we can do this, and you're asking what?"

"It's a lot of real-estate so we're asking $5,000 which includes the bank's real-estate fee."

Randy thinks about it and says, "can Amy and I take a few minutes to discuss it?"

Stepping on the porch, Amy says, "that seems to be a fair price, what do you think?"

"It's more than fair, unless I'm mistaken this house is worth a lot more—probably in the $7,000 range. Basically, this is a deal we can't walk away from."

Stepping back in the dining room, Amy says, "I know that it's not good business to accept the first offer without negotiating. But in this case, you're offering a very fair deal. We'll gladly take it and transfer you the funds today."

***

At the end of the day, while alone in their bedroom, Randy says, "we have the bases for our enterprise. We have our home, our factory and plenty of oil-bearing land. Tomorrow, we start. . . . .

Amy interrupts and says, that's enough talk, let's get into the business of filling that nursery. heh!"

***

CHAPTER 12

BUILDING A HOLSTER FACTORY.

The next morning, after a replenishing breakfast, the duo headed to the factory. Standing at the entrance and looking at the empty structure, Amy says, "where do we start?"

"Go back to your book on Chapter 7—how to build an assembly line. We need to build tables for workers. The bench against the wall will be a continuous one. The bench against the center posts will have several breaks so workers can step out of the line. We are not building anything on the right side of the factory. That is reserved for a second assembly line in the future.

So, let's go visit Ken Learman's construction company to get these benches built."

While the carpenters were busy with the project, the duo went to see Harvey Samuels at his leather shop. On entering, Harvey grabbed Amy and gave her a big hug. "We all heard you were back and bought the old stagecoach factory. What are you up to?"

After introducing Randy, Amy said, "first, tell me what you're up to?"

"Getting older, I decided I needed a change. I sold all my saddlery leather, accessories and tools. I'm left with holster grade leather and tools to make holsters. I'm really scratching to make a living supplying the local gun shops with holsters. I don't have the energy to expand beyond Amarillo. So, it is what it is, heh?"

"Harvey, I'm building a holster factory. Sell me your leather inventory and all the tools in your shop. Then, come to work for me as my shop foreman. The workers will be offered 20 cents an hour, or $1.60 per 8-hour day—that's $8 per week. I'll pay you $30 a week and after we train the workers, you can work the number of days a week you want."

"My goodness, that's twice the money I'm presently scratching out of this shop, and a lot less hours. Jim Westland next door has been after me to sell him the shop so he can expand. Would you pay me $1,000 for the entire contents of the shop?

"Harvey, that's a third of what it's worth."

"Yeah but, who else would want to buy it?"

"Ok, we have a deal. Work starts in two days. Here is your $1,000 voucher. We'll start moving equipment tomorrow."

"What's next?"

"We need workers. Let's go to Harper's Mercantile and place a help wanted ad on the bulletin board. We'll also send a telegram to Houston and ask the telegrapher to post our 'help wanted ad' on the town bulletin board. We'll start interviews in four days."

After placing an ad, they asked Sylvio Harper if he had catalogs on leather working tools. "Yes, I ordered this one after Harvey showed interest in modernizing his equipment.

If you are interested, go see Maitland Anisson, he's a mechanical engineer who can power these tools with a steam engine."

During lunch at Suzie's Diner, the duo studied the catalog and skipped dessert to rush to Mr. Anisson's office.

"Hello, what can I do for you?"

"Can you power Harvey Samuels leather tools to a power source as well as these tools in this catalog?"

"Certainly, I can power the new tools, I'd have to see Harvey's tools before I commit on them!"

"Great, can you come to check out Harvey's tools and see our factory today before we order these new tools"

"Let's go, I'm ready."

After seeing Harvey's tools and the factory, it was clear that harnessing new tools to a steam plant was easy. Maitland suggested that Harvey's tools be left as they are, using mechanical manpower. These tools would be a backup if ever the steam plant was down for repairs. Maitland chose the machine models that could be harnessed to steam. These included: buffing, sewing, cutting, punching, rivet setting, tooling and engraving. A steam plant was ordered along with all the accessories to harness the tools.

When interviews started, Harvey was the first line of defense. Harvey knew everyone in town and was able to wean out the drunks, the troublemakers, and the incapable workers. His job was to prepare a list of honest and respectable people who were willing to learn their job and to work for a day's wages. Harvey was looking for people who would support and reinforce Amy's manufacturing methods and would not be the type to challenge her—for this was Amy's business, not the employees.

Once Harvey finished the screening. He presented the names of three men with leather working experience from Houston. Amy met with the first. He was a newly-wed man whose wife had a one-year college degree in accounting. The young man had been an apprentice in a harness shop and was familiar with the tools of the trade. The couple, Ray and Melinda Harrison, was hired. The wife would become the business accountant to handle payroll, billing, and bookkeeping. The young man would become one of her managers. To get him to move to town, sooner than later, Amy gave him a $100 voucher incentive to help the couple find housing. Unfortunately, the other experienced leather worker from Houston had buffaloed his way thru Harvey. Amy saw an arrogant know it all personality that would not work out.

The third man, Eric Greenwood, was only eighteen years old but had worked an apprentice year in a leather shop making scabbards, saddlebags and saddles. He was polite and very reserved. Amy asked him if he had the patience to do fine engraving and tooling as well as fill in for any sick worker. His answer will always stay with Amy, "Ma'am I'll do any job you wish me to do, and if I don't know how to do it, I'll learn. I may be young, but I'll give you 110% and years of service." Again, with Harvey's approval, he too was hired as a manager.

With Harvey as shop foreman and two managers willing to do fine detailed work and or fill in any sick worker's table, Amy needed to hire ten assembly line workers. As agreed, Romeo would be the general support man for the shop and Suzanne and Stella would be in receiving, packing, and shipping orders.

Amy had 31 general laborer applicants and was planning to hire 10 for the first crew. She interviewed all 31 over three days and came out with three groups—hire now, waiting list, and would not fit in this shop.

Of the "hire now" group were four women and six men. The women were given the finer jobs such as leather buffing, tracing patterns, finishing belts with hardware and sewing ammo loops, and Amy's engraving assistant.

The six men were given hardier jobs to include: hand and power cutting, leather dyeing, heavy duty sewing, punching holes, rivet and Concho setting, and edge tooling.

***

For the next two weeks the shop was set up by Maitland and his crew. All tools were set up and powered by the new steam plant installed in its own shed. Amy confirmed that each tool was operating as it was expected.

When everything was operational, Amy generated a sample holster of the ones the shop would produce. During the manufacturing, with Maitland watching, all the kinks were removed from the machinery. These finished holsters included:

1. Standard belt holster.
2. Pommel holster.
3. Standard cross draw holster.
4. Buscadero rig—plain and deluxe (rig includes belt).
5. Gunfighter deluxe rig (rig includes belt).
6. Shoulder holster for mini pistol.
7. Ranger and taper-tongue belts.

When the entire batch of holsters was completed, Randy brought an artist from the Amarillo Gazette, to make designs that the newspaper printing press could reproduce.

Over the next 10 days, two teams trained ten positions on the assembly line. The instructors were Harvey with Ray, and Amy with Eric. Each day they taught one holster until everyone could do their job before moving the holster to the next table for another process or addition. By the time the holster started on station one (the dyeing table) to the last station, a new holster was produced. The deluxe models were slower than the standard ones but were worth more money.

After ten days of training, Randy said, "in the first days of operation, your staff produced a plain holster every 15 minutes and a deluxe rig every 30 minutes. Eventually, this shop has to be efficient enough to put out a mix of either holsters or belts every 5 minutes. That's 12 pieces every hour or about 100 pieces a day."

Amy added, "we'll be able to meet that goal. Now that's 500 pieces a week, where are we going to sell all that?"

"Not to worry, marketing is my job and I have it under control. Just make the product and I'll sell them."

***

Meanwhile Randy had been working with the printer at the Gazette. He just generated his first flyer that advertised The McWain Holster Company. The flyer included a reproduction of all their products and their prices. A second flyer had an order form and a condition of sale statement. Randy ordered 500 copies of each and went to visit with the town clerk.

The town clerk had been working on this project for several weeks. When Randy walked in, the clerk had everything ready. "As you requested, the state offices for Texas, Colorado and New Mexico had the information you requested. Texas has 72 registered gun shops, Colorado 69 and New Mexico has 59. The names and addresses are all included in these copied sheets. The fees are $15 for the copying department to duplicate the original lists. So, you owe the town $45 since our office had to pay the copying fee beforehand."

"Here is the $45 plus your fee of $25."

"you don't have to pay me, it's part of my job."

"Nonsense, now that we have the west-northwest addresses, let's do the same for east-northeast gun shops in Louisiana, Arkansas, Missouri and Kansas. At the same time, can you get me addresses of mercantiles from towns of over 500 people that don't have a local gun shop."

"Can do, but the mercantile addresses may take longer."

"That's ok, we have nearly 200-gun shop addresses to start with. Here is a down payment of $200 for the estimated copying fees and your fee of $50."

The next day, Randy went back to the Gazette and picked up the flyers that were ready. He also ordered another 500 of both flyers. He also picked up 1,000 envelopes and 2 cent postage stamps. Arriving at the shop, Randy explained to Melinda, the office secretary and accountant, what he wanted. "Here are the three lists of gun shops in three states, each one gets a product flyer and an order form/condition of sale add-on."

Melinda checks out the product flyer and order form. She added a smile and said, "very professional." Amy looks at the flyers and also adds a smile.

"I especially like the condition of sale ad-on, as she read out loud. Condition of Sale:

1. All orders must include a payment in full by bank draft.
2. Shipping is included to the nearest railroad depot.
3. Buyer is responsible for arranging delivery to place of business from the railroad depot.
4. Only minimum orders of $50 will be accepted to qualify for these wholesale prices.
5. Product satisfaction is guaranteed or return for full refund."

When Randy explained what he was doing, he added, "This is the first round of advertising. The second round will include states to the east-northeast. The third round will include mercantiles from towns without a gun shop but have a population of 500 or more."

Amy was impressed, adding, "that's great marketing, I suspect we have several weeks to continue building our inventory before the orders start coming in. These three advertising rounds will likely keep us busy for a long time, what have you got in your magic hat for the future?"

"I already have an idea for the future, but first, I need to see how productive this current marketing ploy works out."

***

The next week, Randy watched the assembly line to see if he could add some beneficial tips. The workers were working independently and knew what they needed to do. The problem was that they would work all day making one holster. That method was efficient, and they were putting out a holster every 5 minutes. However, orders would be coming in with several models, for either a Colt or S&W pistol and for different barrel lengths. It was clear that a new system was needed.

Working on this conundrum was Amy,

Randy, Harvey, Melinda, Suanne and Stella. After several suggestions failed, it was Randy's mom, Stella, who came up with a winner.

"I have an idea, try this one. Every holster has a tag with a code such as 12—2-4AR-3.

"Please explain."

"The number 12 is the sequential number of a gun shop's order up to 1000, which is needed for me to pack and ship. The number 2 stands for the one of four leather colors—in this case it is black. The number 4 stands for one of our seven models—in this case it is a gunfighter holster. The letter A stands for a Colt and the letter B for a S&W. The letter R stands for right hand, L for left hand holster. The number 3 stands for one of four barrel lengths available—in this case it is a 51/2 inch barrel. Technically, if all tag specs are followed, the holster produced should be as ordered."

Amy was first to comment. "So, each holster has a tag with this code system. Each worker already knows what he needs to do for a holster coming down the assembly line with these specifications. If he can't remember his job, it can be written down on a sign posted on his wall."

Stella added, "when this revolver arrives at the end of the assembly line, it's up to Suzanne to verify that the product matches with the tag order. Since the customer number is documented. This holster will be automatically packaged off the assembly line."

Randy added, "there is only one weak link to this system. If the person making the tag order screws up, then the product is not what the customer ordered."

Stella thought a bit and came back, "with the product guarantee you provide with each order, maybe two people should independently prepare the tags to get a match before it goes to the assembly line."

Amy finally settled the issue. "I like this system, after the break I will present it to the staff. Let's start with Stella and Melinda preparing the tags. That way, we'll not only catch errors, but if one of you cannot come to work, we can still operate. With this system, the tag maker controls production."

"Until we get orders, let's start the code system now to continue building our inventory and train our staff."

For the next two weeks, Stella and Melinda were generating tags that helped fill all the missing holsters in the inventory. It was Melinda that was keeping track of the total numbers. It shocked Randy when he was told that they had 2,000 holsters and 500 belts on hand.

Finally, the first orders arrived. Romeo would pick up the mail by 2PM and the tags were prepared for the next morning. When the tags were all manufactured, the inventory tags would finish the day. The first orders amounted to 69 products. Since the shop could put out 100 products per day, by 3PM, the inventory tags came out to finish the day. The second day's orders came to 88 products and that was the last day the total day's orders were less than 100 products.

For weeks, the shop was running at maximum production. Despite this, the shop could not keep up with the orders. At one point, the shop was behind 500 products. That's when Amy authorized Suzanne and Stella to fill orders out of the inventory. A month later, they were behind another 500 products, and the inventory was tapped for the second time. The duo decided it was time to utilize the other half of the shop and build a second assembly line—but told no one.

Before implementing their plans, the duo scheduled a meeting to review finances and statistics. Present at the meeting were Melinda, Romeo, Suzanne, Stella, Ray, Eric, Harvey and the duo. Melinda started presenting the starting expenses, cost of wages, cost of materials, and unexpected/miscellaneous expenses. The total figure was a bit daunting. Then Melinda reviewed the income per the three states, Texas, Colorado and New Mexico. It became clear that at the end of four months, the business was in the black. What Randy saw was that current statistics showed a third was for materials, a third for labor, and a third was now going to be profit.

The meeting's second half was statistics. As expected, the least popular holster was the pommel holster but still worth keeping on. The most popular was the buscadero rig. The standard, cross draw and gunfighter rig were selling in equal numbers. The most popular leather color was black. The real shocker was the shoulder harness for a mini pistol which was the #2 seller. Melinda pointed out that these shoulder holsters came from the larger cities where wearing a sidearm was being replaced by the less obvious firearm under a coat or vest.

Once Melinda was done, Amy opened the floor to questions. Harvey started, "the toughest job on the line is the first man who is breaking his back, dyeing hides. To make it worse, he has to doubly dip the black otherwise he generates a grey color. This man needs help."

Amy responded, the next time you see a need, it's your right as shop foreman to hire more help without asking permission. I'm giving you the waiting list, work from the top and get that man a helper."

Romeo was next. "One buys a loaf of bread this week and needs to buy another next week. Holsters are not like bread. They are durable and last for decades. Things are going well with orders now, but when things begin to slow down, how are you going to keep the pace up?"

Randy answered by discussing his plans for round two and three of the mailing marketing strategies. Round two is being addressed by Melinda, Suzanne and Stella. The mailing would be on its way within a few days.

Suzanne was next, "how do we know if the buyers are satisfied with our product?"

Melinda answered. "We are already getting repeat orders and several orders include very positive words under the comment section."

Ray was next. "Any chance of adding new models in the near future?"

Amy said, "that depends on when new pistols are developed or when pistols from Europe flood the US market. There is the likelihood that bulky double action pistols are coming which will require a new holster. For now, we continue our present models."

Eric was last to enter the arena. He said, "I have three issues. The first is the fact that we are missing some great ideas to make this business better. Your experienced workers can contribute. We need a suggestion box and a bonus system to compensate for money saving ideas. Secondly, I work with the men and women and can attest that everyone is working above their max. Everyone, including me, goes home quite tired. And third we can't keep up with the orders. Isn't it time to add a second assembly line?"

Silence fell upon the room until Randy came alive and said, "well Eric, you just took our thunder away. Amy and I had come to that conclusion yesterday. That is why we called this meeting. Starting tomorrow I'll be ordering new tools and working with Maitland to power them. Harvey, you'll be on the employment committee with Amy. Ray and Eric, talk to the workers and arrange for the next assembly line work benches to incorporate the workers ideas. Dad and both moms, decide how much help you'll need and the hours you wish to work. Melinda, please arrange for the construction company to start building the assembly line and find a 'box' company who can supply us with our expected expansion. Also, check with our leather supplier. Can they increase their deliveries, or do we add a second supplier?"

The second line interviews started and most of Harvey's waiting list, from the original hiring, were referred to Amy for final consideration. There were two surprises and an unexpected high number of applicants. The first surprise was the high number of other factory workers who wanted a side change to leatherworks, including the master stitcher from the shoe and boot factory. The other surprise was Tim from the line one station 6-punching station. His point was that George, from the rivet setting station 5 on line one and he, agreed that these stations should be combined into one since each station by itself did not have enough work to do. Tim would move to line 2 and George would stay on line 1 and both men would do both jobs without holding up the assembly line.

Harvey did a great job in witling down the applications to thirty people referred to Amy. The first two new hires were Tim and the master stitcher from the shoe/boot factory.

The others were all new people that were trainable in leather works and many were from the old waiting list. Amy ended up with 15 new employees and a waiting list of ten new hopefuls.

During the weeks to follow, the wheel was in motion and things got done. With the routine of setting up the tools and manning the assembly line now being second nature, the second line went into full operations. Other than the usual 10 workers on the line, several new positions were filled. Melinda hired two assistants to help Suzanne and Stella. Amy got a new assistant, since her assistant, Miranda, was made in charge of the second line's engraving department and also given an assistant. The worker running the dyeing station was given a helper.

Melinda was the only shared worker. She would work with Suzanne on line 1 to set up the tag codes from half the orders. Then she would work with Stella on line 2 to handle the other half of orders and set up the tag codes.

This double check system finally proved to be foolproof—orders got filled without errors.

With orders coming in regularly and line one working independently, Ray, Harvey and Eric were free to work with the new workers on line two.

One day Amy found the first comment in the suggestion box. It was line 1 stitcher who wrote, "it's time that we develop a company logo to stamp on all our products, and as we approach 1890, we need to develop our own trademark holster with new innovations to include molded holsters to fit the Colt Peacemaker—signed Billy at station 8.

Amy reread the note and finally pulled the steam whistle to make an announcement. "Billy just made a suggestion which I like. He'll get a bonus in his paycheck. Now the suggestion is that we need our own trademark holster with innovations. Billy's suggestion was to add our first molded holster. For every innovative suggestion we accept, I will give you a bonus equal to a week's pay. You have till tonight to get your ideas in the suggestion box."

During the day, Melinda was astonished to see the number of line 1 workers walk up to the suggestion box and make a deposit. After the 5PM whistle blew and the shop emptied, Melinda brought the suggestion box to Harvey and the duo. Amy opened each one and read the note as Randy was making a list of suggestions. The list included:

- A fold-over, double stitch, open toe black holster
- A cut down front to ease a quick draw
- A 5-degree forward muzzle cant for natural wrist positioning
- A flared-out top or rolled out edge for easy holstering
- An angled-out holster top to push holster away from the belt
- A belt loop to allow holster sliding for individual positioning
- 2-6-inch holster drop below belt to compensate for arm length
- Maintain an exposed trigger guard to fix gun on holster stitching

- Mold the Colt to the buscadero rig and call it the 'lawman special'"

Harvey was first to make a comment. "I think we can make all the suggested modifications to the gunfighter rig except the holster molding. The gunfighter draw would be slowed by molding the holster to the gun. However, by molding the buscadero rig to a Colt, it will ease the draw which is now too tight in the existing model. The new gunfighter rig could be called the 'deluxe' model. Both these new models should replace the old models, thereby not confusing our assembly lines."

Randy looked at Amy for her thoughts on the matter. "I have nothing to add. I like what I hear, and we can accomplish this by modifying the assembly lines. So that means that we are going to need some molds. We'll need a Colt pistol mold and a top/bottom setting mold for the buscadero rig, and a mold to make the flared-out top of the gunfighter rig. Where do we get these molds fabricated?"

"I will talk to Maitland for some suggestions

and get back to you. Are we going to order some special leather for molding?"

"No, we would use the vegetable tanned top grain leather in 8 ounces."

"That was a mouthful, can you explain these specs to me?"

"Full grain leather comes from the top or back of the hide and in its natural form, is rough and full of natural fibers for strength and used to make harnesses. For holsters, we use top grain leather, which is thinner, softer and smooth. It comes from the edge of the hide and is sanded to remove fibers to get a smooth surface. The 8 ounce means 8/64 of an inch or 1/8 inch in thickness. The thickness is crucial for molding. Vegetable tanning does not use chemical salts which can corrode guns. We only use vegetable tanned leather in this shop."

The next day, on his way to see Maitland, Randy stopped to see Jim Westland in his gun shop. "Jim I need two Colts, one short and one long, that don't shoot. I have a 4 ¾ inch and a 7 ½ inch that have no internal parts. The bores are shot out from lack of cleaning the corrosive black powder residue. I keep the internal parts for repairs. You can have them at no charge. Now, I have a Colt rep coming tomorrow and I really feel you need to meet with him. He is having trouble selling some new guns, and from our last visit, I think he needs your help."

"Sure, I'll meet with him, but I don't know much about gun sales, I'm still in the learning stages of holster manufacturing."

"Great, be here at noon and we'll all have a luncheon meeting."

His next stop was at Maitland's office. Once he explained what he needed, Maitland said, "Interesting situation. Fortunately, we have a wood working shop in town who have the steam powered machinery to make anything out of the ordinary, and this is certainly out of the ordinary. Let's go and see the shop manager."

Arriving at Amarillo Wood Works, they were greeted by Anson Sweeney. Randy explained what they needed, and Anson answered. "This is doable. We will set up several jigs using the pistols you brought. These jigs will be used to duplicate the parts you need: a pistol mold for 4

¾ in. barrel and one for a 7 ½ in. barrel, a plug for the gunfighter flared-out top, a compression plate for the 'top form' and a compression plate for the 'bottom frame.' We will use hardwoods that do not absorb much water and so won't swell much. The top and bottom compression plates will be drilled to accommodate bolts and nuts to maintain compression. We'll need both pistols to make the molds, and the holsters that need an edge flaring. How many do you want of each?"

"Since this is new to me, let's start with 20 of each piece."

"That's 40 wood pistol molds, 40 compression plates and 20 edge flaring molds. That comes up to $200 and will be ready in a week."

Getting back to the shop, Randy explained what he had ordered. Amy had already started to modify the assembly lines. Amy added, "since very little is known about molding leather holsters, we'll learn by trial and error. The key will be how long the leather will take to dry in the molds."

The next day, as Randy was preparing to go

to his luncheon meeting, Amy asked, "when the suggestions came out yesterday, didn't you have some of your own?"

"Yes, I have three, but this is not the time to add them with all the changes we are making."

"I agree, but what are they so I can think about it."

"We'll eventually want to add some belt slides to hold 44-40 pistol ammo, 45-70 rifle ammo and shotgun ammo. The second is to make clip-on top open leather pouches to hold live and spent ammo while shooting at a range. The third is to make three sizes for the shoulder rig to accommodate small, medium and large mini pistols."

"Ok and I especially agree with the shoulder rig. As times change, the side arm carrying cowboy will change to the gentlemen toting a concealed weapon in a shoulder rig—especially in the cities."

The meeting took place at the Sommerset Hotel's restaurant. Jim introduced the Colt rep as Roger McCarthur from Hartford Connecticut. After drinks and a light lunch of local trout, the meeting started over a pot of coffee. Roger started, "my company is trying to move away from the single action Peacemaker to the new double action pistols. That is where the future of revolvers is heading before the slide semi-automatics join the handgun market. The problem is that these double action pistols just simply don't sell out West. The standard answer is "I wouldn't be caught dead with one of those, or, that's a sissy gun, or, give me a real man's gun—the Colt Peacemaker in either 45Long Colt or 44-40."

"Now out in the East, they sell very well. We have three models now available. The 1877 model comes in three calibers. The 'lightning' is in 38 long Colt, the 'Thunderer' is in 41 Colt and the 'Rainmaker' is in 32 Colt. The second is the 1878 model which is a larger version of the 1877 and fires the 45 Colt cartridge. The current new model is the 1889 model that has a swing out cylinder."

"The problem we are having is that the standard Colt Peacemaker holster does not fit these pistols. The 1877 is too small, the 1878 is too large and the 1889 is odd shape because of the swing out cylinder. A second choice for a holster is the generic box type that ruins the appearance of a side arm. Several private leather men have produced their own version, but that's not the overall solution. We need a unique holster for each pistol to help the sales along and the customers are demanding it. The universal comment we get is, 'I love the pistol but hate wearing it in public with that ugly holster.'"

Randy is handling and examining each pistol as he adds, "I can see why you have issues. Each of these models needs its own holster designed to fit the gun and highlight its shape. The holster needs to follow the pistol's contour and sit on a wide apron for stability on the hip. It should have a two-inch drop below the belt and made of soft/smooth top grain leather for wearing comfort. All our holsters are open toe to prevent debris from plugging the barrel."

"If I could see a prototype for each pistol, that appeals to me, I'd be ready to make an order of 1,000 holsters. I have several gun shops to visit in north Texas and can be back in one week."

"I'll need the three pistols for a week and let my wife with her talent become creative. We'll both see what she comes up with."

Getting back to the shop, Amy looked at the three pistols and agreed with Randy's choice of specs but added she would put some special touches to the final product. Amy mentioned, "I've already designed the new buscadero and gunfighter rigs, but we can't start till we get those wooden molds. So, I have the week to design these three holsters which may mean a large order and profit."

A week later Amy presented Randy, with a big smile, the three holsters with the pistols in the holsters. The holsters were in brown, burgundy and black to match the guns. Each holster was cut and shaped in a unique fashion that enhanced the pistol's appearance. I was a work of art. Randy added, "wife, you are a genius. And to think you did it all yourself. Now I'm convinced you're really happy, because in your case, it's not just doing what you like, but it's liking what you do, heh."

"That was the nicest thing you could say, now go land a contract and you'll have special attention from me tonight."

Randy walked into the Westland gun shop and put all three holstered pistols on the counter. Roger stood there with an astonished frozen look on his face. He kept moving his eyes from one holster to another and it was clear that he couldn't believe what he was looking at.

"Goodness gracious, I never believed that an appropriate holster could make such a difference. This is craftsmanship at his best. How much do you want for 1,000 holsters—333 of each?"

"$6,000."

"Done and I'll pay the train freight. How long to get them?"

"They'll be on the train in one week, and you'll get them in Hartford in 9 days. That's the railroad's schedule to cover 1,800 miles."

"If this promotion goes well, I'll be back for another order."

When Randy arrived with a contract, Amy

was jumping around like a kid. How did you choose the amount of $6,000? That is more than we usually get for a profit margin."

"This is a special and custom order that interrupts our shop schedule. We can set our own profit margin for such an order. Besides, Roger was more than pleased to pay $6 per holster, knowing he would charge $9 in Hartford and Boston. Things are bigger in Texas but more expensive in Connecticut or Massachusetts, heh!"

"Ok, the molds are not ready, so let's get going on this order."

***

CHAPTER 13

DRILLING FOR OIL

Within seven days, the Colt custom order was on its way. The wooden molds arrived, and Amy established a method for molding the buscadero rig. The holster was soaked in warm to hot water, then preliminarily hand molded to the wood pistol mold, before compressing it in the double molded hardwood blocks. Tightening the bolts, the compressed holster was set aside for four hours and then allowed to air dry overnight as the molds were then used on the next holster.

The gunfighter holster had a simpler molding step. With the holster's edge wet, the edge was rolled back manually, and held there by inserting the secured wooden plug for the same time period. Like the buscadero rig, both holsters were molded a day ahead of time. That meant a new employee was hired to do this job from day to day, and it took him eight hours to prepare 200 holsters to maintain the assembly line's production schedule.

After going to the Gazette, a new flyer was designed by the artist to display the new gunfighter and buscadero rigs for 1890. With a sample in hand, Melissa was given the task of mailing it to every gun shop and mercantile in the adjoining states—using the same lists used in the first four mailings.

Since the special order of Colt holsters had put the shop behind, and now the new mailings, Randy realized that he was free to start working on his oil project. To start, he went to see his favorite mechanical engineer, Maitland Annison.

"Good morning, what brings you here today?"

"Oil. Tell me what you know."

"Oil is the future of this country. It can make you wealthy or bankrupt. First, you need land that has prospects."

"I've got three lots totaling 18,000 acres and all within five miles of each other. These all have extensive surface seeping oil pools, and I have complete mineral rights."

"That puts you over the first hurdle. Now, we can presume that your land sits over the same oil reservoir. However, it doesn't mean that the three lots have the same drilling depths to reach the oil. The earthen roof over the reservoir can vary by thousands of feet from the surface. So, if the first well hits oil at 500 feet, it means nothing for the other lots."

"Is it possible to drill to the maximum depth of your drilling company and not hit oil?"

"Of course, drilling for oil is a speculative investment. Until you hit the oil reservoir, you have nothing. I know you have hundreds of questions, but I think it's time to speak to an oil man. I have a college friend who is in the oil drilling business. I happen to know he uses the state-of-the-art rotary drilling system and is currently finished drilling a well. Let's take a buggy ride to his office and talk with Cliff Tilton."

***

"Cliff, this is Randy McWain of McWain Holsters. He has promising land and is considering drilling for oil."

"Great, let me give you my standard information and then I will answer your questions. The first thing I do is drill for water and set up a windmill pump. The water is used to extracts the drilled dirt and stone chips. Without water, I don't set up for drilling. At this point, you have no investment, the water well and windmill are on me."

With an adequate water supply, we sign a contract. I erect a massive derrick that stands forty feet high used to hold the drill bit and drive pipes. I charge $25 per foot of drilling in dirt that requires a drive pipe to prevent collapse of earth in the bore. Once I hit bedrock, the drive pipe is no longer needed, and I drill 500 feet at the same rate. If we drill beyond 500 feet, the price goes up to $40 per foot. I can drill as deep as 1,000 feet. If we don't hit oil, the cost may bankrupt you."

"Historically, how deep are current wells in north or west Texas?"

"For what it's worth, they presently vary from 100 feet to a thousand feet. But the average is 600 feet."

"What happens once we hit oil?"

"Assuming we hit a gusher, first we cap it as soon as the pressure of the oil flume drops. Then we start cleaning up the oil mess on the ground. Afterwards we set up a series of pipes and valves to collect oil from the primary production. This primary production is generated from high pressure in the reservoir and can last for years. During the primary production, if you can generate 50 barrels a day, you have a money maker on your hands."

"How long can this primary production last?"

"Unknown. It can be months or years. Once the flow stops, we build a pump to extract the oil during the secondary production. This secondary production usually lasts for years."

"What is this pump all about?"

"A 'pumpjack' is basically and elevator to lift the crude oil out of the well. We erect a small derrick that holds a beam called a 'walking beam.' At one end is a heavy weight in the shape of a horse's head. The rear end of the beam has a steam powered plant, that turns the rotating eccentric weighted wheel into vertical movement of the beam, to lift oil out of the well. Because the entire structure looks like a perpetually moving horse, the 'pumpjact' is called a 'nodding donkey.'"

"During the primary production, I dismantle the drilling derrick for future use. Once the secondary production starts, I build the pumpjack for a fee of $2,000. By the time the secondary production starts, you'll be a rich man."

"There is one last issue. I won't start unless I have reassurances from your investors that my work will be covered financially irrelevant of the outcome."

"That's reasonable. In this case, there are no investors. Take this note to the bank and show it to President Greathouse. He will show you my account's balance. When can you start?"

"Sign a contract, and I'll start digging for a water well tomorrow."

"Done. Now Maitland, is this something you'd be interested to get involved with?"

"Yes, things are slow for a mechanical engineer in town. I would love to be involved from the beginning."

"Well let me place you on retainer and you can be on the job starting tomorrow. You'll be my voice when I'm not on the job and you can explain things to me when I am there."

"Let's all meet behind the Craymore homestead tomorrow morning and I'll bring you to the drilling site."

***

Arriving on horseback it became clear that wagons and buggies would have an easy time to get to the drill site. Cliff approved the site and kept saying, "I've never seen so much surface oil.

It is clear that cracks in the bedrock are filling up from high pressures in the reservoir. When we hit a gusher, it's going to be a monster one."

Within days, the Tilton crew had a well and windmill up. The pressure was way above what was the minimum flow to extract drilling chips. The next step was erecting a derrick. Precut and drilled 4X6 inch beams were trucked in. The beams were secured with large dowel pins for reuse. In a matter of a week, the derrick was up and reached 45 feet. Drilling rods and drive pipes were brought in by freight wagons. After securing them to the derrick, drilling was about to start.

During this entire preparatory work, Randy and Maitland were present. They were impressed how well the Tilton crew was working out. As the drilling started, Amy even showed up and was given the grand tour. Amy had many questions especially as the drilling started. Everyone was amazed how fast the rotary drill went thru earth. The next step was to pull the drill out and drive a massive 20-foot pipe in the hole to prevent collapse of the earthen bore.

After another 20 feet a second drive pipe was added and coupled with a union onto the previous pipe. Now both 20-foot were driven down the hole. By the end of the day, reaching 75 feet, the drill hit solid bedrock. The extra five foot of pipe was cut off and preparations for bedrock drilling were started.

Amy was getting in the swing of things as she said, "at $25 a foot, these 75 feet cost us $1,875. Now in bedrock what affects the drilling speed?"

Maitland answered, "the type of rock is the major factor. Soft porous rock is easy drilling whereas granite is a nightmare. Usually we have rock hardness in-between. The other factor is depth of drilling. When you're drilling at 500 feet, and you have to replace the drilling bit, that requires days to remove the 20-foot drilling rods to get to the drill bit. Also drilling at 500 feet puts the entire system at a mechanical disadvantage."

"I don't understand this mechanical disadvantage."

"Imagine twirling a large umbrella with a three-foot handle. Now do the same with a

500-foot handle. It will take all your energy to rotate the handle and the umbrella will barely be turning."

"Oh, I see. So, time and examining the rock chips will tell us the bedrock's consistency and hardness."

"Yes, and that information can change as the bedrock changes."

"So, the slow step of bedrock drilling starts as well as the long anxiety producing waiting period, heh."

***

For several days, Randy stayed at the drilling site. Realizing that the process was proceeding at 10 feet per day, Randy lost patience with the wait. It was Maitland who suggested that Randy needed to prepare for the day the well came in. "How do I do that?"

"Let's assume this well comes in and you get a monster gusher that takes several days for Cliff's crew to cap. How are you going to clean the mess, and what are you going to do with the oil if the primary production is 50-100 barrels a day? Oh, let's not forget where you'll put these full barrels, since you don't have any barrels, heh!"

"Oh my, I'd better start making some arrangements. Yet, how do I make arrangements when I don't even know if my well will hit oil."

"You're not the only independent digging for oil. Cliff says that these companies accept a small deposit and the order is only filled if the well comes in. If it doesn't come in, 50% of your deposit is refundable."

"Where do I get wooden barrels? Where do I hire heavy equipment for the cleanup? What kind of storage facility do I need."

"I know the owner/operator of steam powered plowing tractors and steam shovels. I will put them on hold and there is no charge."

"Now oil barrels are not a simple matter. A producing oil well needs a basic supply of available wooden barrels. Wooden barrels are made of oak and are convex shaped with a central bulge called the 'bildge.' They hold 42 gallons of crude oil and weigh full at 300 pounds. These are leak proof since the pieces of wood, staves, are kept in place by steel hoops. Each barrel will cost you $1 but will be reusable for years till the steel barrel is manufactured in the years to come."

"Why are the barrels convex with a 'bildge.'"

"For strength since an arched bridge is stronger than a straight one. Also, with a central bildge, it makes it easier to roll and maneuver a barrel on the ground, heh?"

"Where do I get wooden barrels and what kind of storage should I plan for?"

"Out of Missouri where there are plenty of oak trees and several plants in operation. Now storage can vary. You could leave the barrels outside and, on the ground, but storage out of the elements is a long-term investment that will pay off. Build a post and beam storage shed with a roof and a wooden floor. That way the wooden barrel's base won't swell from ground moisture and start popping steel hoops which will lead to leaking oil. When the steel barrels take over, they won't rust from the moist ground. These barrels will be with you for years and if you sell some oil, the buyer will give you a replacement or return the empty barrels."

"What size shed are we talking about?"

"Cliff suggested the standard 250 feet long by 50 feet wide. That is 12,500 square feet. A barrel's diameter roughly measures 2 by 2 feet or 4 square feet. Now, 12,500 divided by 4 equals +-3,125 barrels on the first layer and the same on the second layer. So, with access rows, you can store at least 6,000 barrels."

"Now, you don't build the entire structure from the start. You start with a smaller building and keep extending it as the barrels fill up. For now, talk to Ken Learman's Construction about starting to accumulate some posts and beams from local mills."

"Ok, tomorrow I'll start sending letters, telegrams and telegraph vouchers. I'll also make arrangements with Ken."

***

For several weeks, Randy stayed away from the drill site. Each night, on his way home, Maitland had the same answer, "the drilling is going well, did 11 feet today but the drilling chips are not showing any signs of oil." His current total was 75 feet with a drive pipe and 152 feet of bedrock drilling—now worth some $5,500 plus $2,000 for the derrick.

To pass the time, Randy went to the shop to help Melinda send out the new mailing that included the deluxe gunfighter rig and the molded buscadero rig. To Randy's surprise the flyer also included the ammo slides and the clip-on leather pouches he had recommended. Melinda had been at it for a week and appreciated Randy's help. Randy would stuff the envelopes with the flyers, add a postage stamp, and wet the glue with a sponge to seal them. Every day, the batch was brought to the post office for mailing. It was five days later that the mailing was complete, and Randy said, "hopefully, this extensive mailing will maintain the shop for the next year."

Amy was listening and asked, "if it doesn't keep us going, what is your next marketing strategy?"

"We'll have to devise a way to start

advertising in the East, and start including holsters for the new revolvers coming out from Colt, S&W. and the new gun manufacturers all over Connecticut and Massachusetts. As you know, I'm still working on this one."

With no new news from the drill site, Randy decided to work on advertising out East. Walking into the land office/town clerk, he asked Mo Hancock, "Mo, how can I advertise our holsters out East without doing these labor intense and expensive mailings?"

"I'll show you the answer, and if you agree, you owe me $20, heh?

"Heck, if you have the answer, I'll give you twice that amount."

"Deal. Do you agree to follow my orders?"

"To the word."

"Very good, now go out back to the privy and sit on the hole till you find the answer."

Randy gave Mo the silliest look but followed his direction. After some time sitting in solitude, looking around and thinking, a smile came on Randy's face followed by the loudest laughter that carried him back to the land office. Randy throws two $20 double eagles on the counter and holds one up as he says, "This must seal your lips forever, especially from Amy!"

"Agree, but only if you eventually make her take the same trip into common sense reality, heh?"

That night, Randy was actually giddy, when he thought about his visit with Mo. Amy could see that there was something going on, but Randy was quiet as a church mouse, except for the occasional outburst of laughter. Thankfully, Maitland was arriving with his usual evening report. "Boss, there is a change, at 175 feet in the bedrock, the rock chips are showing signs of oil staining. Cliff feels you and Amy should start the vigil and hopefully the oil signs will get more promising."

The next morning, the duo was at the site waiting for Cliff. He explained, "my past experience is that there are serial changes that occur before the gusher is released. The rock chips will start feeling oily and smell of oil. Then the water flushing the rocks out will start getting an oil slick. Now this may mean we are close to erupting in the reservoir, or it may mean that there are cracks in the bedrock that are spilling oil in the hole. The latter can mean many more feet to the reservoir, or worse."

"We understand. Getting a gusher would be the event of a lifetime, so we'll now stay and wait. We don't want to miss it. Harvey is in charge of the shop and so we have nothing else to do but wait."

The hours passed and the signs were getting better by the hour. At 1PM, Cliff came to announce, "we just got a gush of pure oil instead of the circulating water. In addition, the rock is getting softer from imbibing oil. Get ready, I think we'll be hitting oil within hours."

Every hour became a nerve-racking sixty minutes. Suddenly Amy said, "did you feel that?" Both Randy and Maitland shrugged their shoulders in the negative. A few minutes later there was a clear shuddering of the ground like an earthquake. The shaking stopped and momentary silence followed. Out of nowhere, a soft roar started like a freight train was getting closer and closer. Just as the roar was peaking in intensity, it suddenly stopped, and a massive black plume of oil came gushing out of the well's mouth. The crude oil was shooting up the derrick around the drilling gear and cresting some 50 feet above the derrick. Every man was screaming out and punching the sky as the black mud start falling on their heads. Within minutes, Randy and Amy were dripping wet with oil and standing in oil puddles. They hugged and danced around as Amy said, "I never doubted for a moment that you wouldn't succeed. I just knew you'd become an 'oil man.'"

It was several hours later that the gusher's pressure diminished to a level that allowed Cliff's crew to cap the well. Cliff later admitted that current technology changes allowed a quicker capping.

For the next week the clean-up started. Cliff's crew was steam cleaning the derrick before tearing it down. Maitland was beginning to build the pipes and valves needed to collect crude oil from the primary production. With the oil mess at the well, he was able to fabricate the oil recovery system in his shop and would be able to bring it to the site once the well's mouth and platform had been steam cleaned.

The grounds were scraped clean by the steam powered tractor while the steam shovel was busy digging a massive hole surrounded by mounds of retaining dirt. The oily mud was moved into the center of the hole by the steam shovel and the retaining walls were left untouched. Once the grounds were cleaned, Ken arrived with his lumber and crew, and started building the storage shed. Phase one was 50 feet wide and 50 feet long. The width would remain the same, but phase 2 and 3 would be adding the length. The 2,500 sq. ft shed would cost $1,250 or 50 cents per sq. ft.

The Missouri barrel company was quick to fill out the initial order of 3,000 barrels. It was a slow process since a flat car only carried 20 barrels standing up, whereas the enclosed box cars could hold 50 barrels by triple stacking them on their sides. Randy had arranged for the local freight company to bring the barrels from the railroad yard.

At Cliff's suggestion, Randy had ordered a

special flat wagon to transfer oil barrels from the well to the storage shed. Of course, the most important items were the two manual lifts/wagons. One would lift the wood oil barrels and load them to the flat wagon while the other one would lift and unload the full barrel as well as stack it onto the first or second row. Two horses would be kept in a small barn and be used to pull the wagon back and forth.

With the derrick dismantled and hauled away, the last thing Cliff did before leaving the drill site was to help Maitland install the primary production collection system. The six employees were present to be given instructions. Since this oil collection would be a 24-hour job, two men would handle each shift, to collect the oil, load the barrels onto the flat wagon and go stack them in the shed. If the well produced 100 barrels a day, each 8-hour shift would need to manhandle 33 barrels—or 4 per hour.

With the system in full operation, Randy could finally rest knowing that the project was yielding a sellable product. It was Amy who had many questions.

"Why do oil barrels hold 42 gallons instead of the standard 55- gallon barrels?"

"It was a standard adopted years ago. In reality 42 gallons of crude oil weighs 300 pounds—and that's about the limit two men can handle."

"How long can we store crude oil?"

"When the oil comes out of the ground, it is 145 degrees F. Once it seals the barrel, it never goes bad and can be stored indefinitely."

"What are your options after 6,000 barrels are full?"

"Buy more barrels and store them outside, or build another shed, or shut down the well or sell some oil barrels to make room and pay expenses."

"Seems that selling some would be good business."

"That depends on the price per barrel. Today it is $1 per barrel. In a week it can drop or be up to $2.50. The price can vary from day to day."

"What or who controls the price."

"Right now, Standard Oil is the giant that is storing large amounts of oil waiting for the price to climb. The distilleries, or refineries as they are being called, coming on-line need crude oil to stay in business, and business depends on the demand for the distilling products."

"So, what are the distilling products?"

"Fractional distillation consists of heating crude oil, and the first by-product at low temperatures is propane which requires bottling. As the temperature climbs the second product is kerosene and gasoline."

"Again, with increasing temperatures, the third product is diesel and heating fuel oil. The last one at very high temperatures is lubricating oil, motor oil and finally asphalt."

"Oh, I see. The automobile is what is delaying the demand."

"Actually, in their need for producing kerosene, refineries only recently stopped dumping unwanted gasoline in rivers. Finally, with the automobile so close, these refineries are now storing gasoline as well as motor oil."

"How much kerosene and gasoline are produced from 42 gallons of crude oil?"

"19 gallons of gasoline and 4 gallons of kerosene."

"So, you're waiting for a refinery to come on-line or an existing one to need crude oil to get the prices up."

"Yes, it also means that Standard Oil has to continue hoarding and the refinery is willing to pay for freight from the storage shed. An alternative is for the refinery to pay the freight company to haul the recently filled barrels directly to the railroad cars and bypass the storage shed. Only time will tell, for now the well is yielding 100 barrels a day, and we are filling the storage shed as fast as Ken is building the additions. No one knows how long the well will keep up this primary production of 100 barrels a day. It could be years or days. For now, my goal is to fill that shed up, and hope the price goes up to $2 a barrel."

"The other thing, now that we're doing well, is to set up a benefactor account at the bank and talk to the Mr. Harper at his mercantile. We need to set up an anonymous donorship to help struggling homesteaders, town's people

304 | Richard M Beloin MD

and ranchers. I don't want anyone to be hungry or lack proper clothing. We have been fortunate and so it's time to start giving some back, heh?"

"I agree. Let's allow Mr. Harper the control over the account since he is the one who knows who needs help."

"I was thinking of asking Mr. Harper to distribute funds to pay for overdue credit accounts, for needs not being attended to such as adequate nutrition and clothing, and for the need of a shotgun to feed themselves by hunting."

"Sounds like we can start the account with a transfer of $5,000 and see how things are going after a few months. In addition, we'll keep this between ourselves, heh?"

***

CHAPTER 14

END OF THE 19TH CENTURY

Times had rolled along and the 1890's were here. The past year had been a profitable one for McWain Leather and Oil. The leather shop had posted a $8,000 profit and Amy's salary was $2,000. The orders were still coming in from the last major mailing to gun shops and mercantiles. Orders were arriving faster than the shop could fill them and so back orders were now three weeks behind. Randy was now certain that the shop's production would never survive his next marketing strategy.

Whereas, McWain Oil had also had a good year. A new refinery had made three 5,000 oil barrel orders at $2 per barrel. They even paid the local freight costs to get the barrels to the railroad depot some three miles away. Empty barrels were being returned on a regular basis. During the year, Randy had paid for the 6,000 barrels, labor, shed construction and miscellaneous expenses. At year's end his oil account had a balance of $18,000.

Randy then said, "Amy, it seems to me that we are at a crucial time with both our businesses. We have plenty of money, your shop can't keep up with orders, and my well is still producing 80 barrels a day. It's time to build a second shop. We need four assembly lines instead of two and I need to drill a second well on Lot #2."

Amy was in partial agreement, "you're half right. It's time to dig your second well. All the economic indicators are predicting an industrial revolution and the commercialization of the automobile. This time, since you're not pressed for time, why don't you use the older and cheaper method of digging an oil well—the chisel type instead of rotary drilling."

"No way, I'm not going back in technology.

The old method consisted of chiseling out the rock by the repetitive lift and drop of the cable/tool kit. This also required stopping the drilling to remove the rock chips. Besides being slow as heck, these rigs don't have other modern technology such as the new methods of capping a gusher. Can you imagine what a mess a five-day gusher would make. No, I'm calling Cliff to move his equipment to Lot #2."

"Guess you're right. Now about the shop's production. The orders will eventually start dropping as they have with other mailings, and we'll catch up on back orders. Let's hold up on construction for now, heh?"

"No. With my next marketing and advertising strategy, you'll be doubling your wholesale orders over night and you'll need that second shop."

"What new marketing ploy do you have in mind?"

"I'm going to let you find out that answer the same way I did. Let's take a ride into town."

Arriving on Main street, they stopped in front of the land office. After tying their horse's reins on the railing, Randy says, "go out back to the privy, and sit there till you find the answer."

Amy gave Randy a strange and suspicious look but decided to comply and entered the privy. Sitting there, Amy waited for an apparition. Randy patiently waited till suddenly he heard Amy yell out "hell yes," as she throws the privy door open and jumps in Randy's arms.

"Mister, you are a genius. Now, how are you going to convince Montgomery Ward to take us on as a holster provider in their catalog?"

"That's for me to know and you to wait to find out. Trust me, you won't be disappointed. I have a secret weapon.

The next day Randy sent a telegraph:

> TO: Winston Montgomery Ward
> Montgomery Ward Catalog dept.
> Chicago, Illinois
> From: Randy McWain
> McWain Holsters
> Amarillo, Texas
> Re: An old favor

Regarding the stagecoach attack
on way to Mineville—STOP
Wife has a holster
company—STOP
Would like to advertise in your
catalog—STOP
Can you help—STOP
<u>Telegram labeled important,</u>
<u>RSVP-- ASAP</u>

Later that day a telegraph messenger arrived
at the shop. Randy gave the messenger two bits
and read:

To: Mr. Randy McWain
How could I forget that
day—STOP
Enclosed is a two-way ticket for
two to Chicago—STOP
Bring samples of all
holsters—STOP
Wire arrival date, will meet you at
train depot—STOP

Before gearing up to take the train. The duo met with Ken Learman's Construction Company regarding the building of a second shop. When informed that they wanted a second shop just like the first one, Ken presented some realistic costs:

Shop 25 X 200=10,000 feet at $1 per = $10,000 sq. ft.

Storage shed, steam plant 20 X = $800 40=800 sq. ft.

Double water closet	= $500
Benches	= $300
Powering tools to steam engine	= $200
Steam engine	= $500
Connecting passageway with doors	= $200
Three heating stoves with pipe chimneys	= $300
Water warming vats in engine room	= $200
Grand Total	=$13,000

PLUS—you buy your own leather working tools

Amy looked at Randy and asked, "how much did we pay for the original building?"

"$11,000 but we added several items to make it functional and $13,000 sounds comparable."

Amy asks, "Ed, how soon can you start?"

"Tomorrow."

Amy gets a nod from Randy and says, "you have a deal. Get started and we'll see you after our return from Chicago."

Over the next few days, Amy gathered every holster the shop manufactured including those with different barrel lengths. She also included samples of ammo slides and clip on leather pouches. She packed them in two large box type luggage and packed their change of clothes in the third piece of luggage. During this time, Randy worked with Ed to set the footings for the shop's and shed's concrete slab.

With the Learman carpenters busy at work and Harvey in charge of the shop, the duo started making arrangements. Amy had to go shopping for an evening dress and Randy had to get a three-piece suit. The only firearms they carried were the Webley Bulldogs—for Randy's shoulder harness and Amy's reticule.

They then sent a telegram to Winston Ward of their expected arrival time and date.

The railroad agent informed them that the trip was 1000 miles long and would likely take at least 33 hours assuming the connections didn't have delays and the train could maintain an average speed of 30 mph. The free tickets courtesy of Mr. Ward, at 3 cents per mile, amounted to a $120 savings. Food services and sleeping arrangements were an extra fee which Mr. Ward had covered.

The trip started and the duo enjoyed watching the landscape. Eventually, they each had purchased and brought the same book to read, Montgomery Ward's "Wish Book" as it was known. Going over some 400 pages of merchandise was a feat in itself. They marveled at the clarity of photographs and the detailed descriptions. The prices seemed lower than the local prices which was a major attraction for customers. It was like walking into a store with every piece of merchandise possible. It included clothing of all types and for different regions of the country. Other items included, farm implements, agricultural tools, hardware, cooking and heating stoves, chimney pipes, buggies, wagons, saddles and tack, bulk dry goods, sewing materials and bolts of fabric, kitchen utensils, carpentry tools, windmills for wells and so many more. Furniture was a big item in the catalog. It included pieces for the kitchen, parlor, bedrooms, office and water closet.

Amy finally commented after getting thru the entire catalog. "Anything you need, whether you live east or west of the Mississippi, is available in this catalog. Isn't that amazing?"

"Yes, and great deals for the consumers. But THERE ARE NO GUNS OR HOLSTERS!"

"I know, but isn't that why we're traveling to Chicago?"

"Certainly is, and I can't wait for our meeting with Mr. Ward."

The meals provided were more than adequate. This included breakfast of scrambled eggs, home fries, biscuits with or without gravy and plenty of coffee. Dinner (noon) was a lavish spread of steak, baked potatoes and choice of other vegetables. Dessert was tapioca pudding with coffee or tea. Snacks were available for supper in the evening.

To the duos surprise, a pullman car was added for nighttime use. The duos ticket included their own private room. The privy was a separate one-holer for either men or women with the deposits falling onto the tracks. The train transfers were done quickly but Randy commented, "I wonder if the luggage cart always gets transferred to the proper destination. I'm glad we're keeping our luggage with us, instead of using the luggage car. I can't imagine getting to Chicago and our holsters went to another city!"

The next day, at 1PM the conductor announced that the Chicago depot was 30 minutes away. As they arrived, Winston Ward was spotted on the receiving platform. When he spotted Randy he said, "hello Mr. McWain and is this your lovely wife?"

"Yes, this is Amy, the master leather crafter, and I'm Randy."

"As I am Winston, bring your luggage and follow me to my carriage. The driver will bring us to the office/warehouse, and we'll be able to talk on the way. Let me give you a synopsis of our company."

"Our founder, Aaron Montgomery Ward started a mail order enterprise with access thru his catalog in the early 70's. The rural customers provided the demand, and we provided the supply. Now in the 1890's we have total sales of 7 million and we send out some 3 million catalogs. Since the present US population is +- 65 million, the potential for growth is incredible."

"Although there are a few minor catalogs around, we have a major competitor coming out with their own catalog—Sears Roebuck. For this reason, we are planning to expand our catalog and we plan to add guns. Holsters would be part of the firearm section. So, your telegram was certainly timely, and besides I owe you a big favor."

Addressing Amy, Winston continued, "that day will remain implanted in my mind forever. For, as the shooting started, I knew that I was going to die. Yet, Randy sat in the stagecoach boot, and without any protection, managed to unhorse most of the outlaws by using shotguns."

Amy put up her hand and added, "say no more, I was on the bounty hunting trail with him for one year, and I know of his crazy antics."

"Well, here we are, let's go to my office to examine your products."

Opening their luggage, they displayed all 18 holsters. They explained each one in detail. They also explained the three double action Colt revolvers they had recently manufactured for Colt.

As Amy explained each holster, Winston placed the holster in his hands to get a better understanding of its purpose. Winston was very impressed with the new deluxe gunfighter and buscadero rigs. After the presentation, Winston looked at the duo and exclaimed, "my goodness, this is craftsmanship at its best. I like what I see. This would be a magnificent addition to our catalog, including the ammo slides and leather clip-on bags. May I make you an offer?"

Randy spoke up, "of course, and there won't be any haggling, we want your business."

"Ok, let's start with your MSRP."

Amy took over, "our standard holsters are $6, our molded ones are $8 and the two deluxe go for $10. What discount would you want?"

"My company charges all vendors the same wholesale discount. 10% plus a handling fee of 5%. The initial order to build our inventory has a surcharge of another 5%. In addition, you pay the railroad freight to get the order to the Chicago railroad depot."

"More than acceptable, don't you agree Amy?" Who nodded yes.

"To build an inventory that is workable, I'll need 50 of each of these 18 holsters. Reorders will be a minimum of 25 holsters per model."

Amy was stunned, "but Sir, that's 900 holsters worth anywhere from $6,000 to $8,000."

"Yes, and once the sales begin, you'll get an order whenever an item goes below 25 holsters. In addition, we pay our vendors within 30 days of receiving an order."

"Now I have another idea. We are planning to sell handguns other than the Colt Peacemaker and the S&W Model 3. We have contracts to include two mini pistols—The Colt Cloverleaf and the S&W 1876. The Remington SA Model 1875 and 1890. The H&R Top Break, Young American, Vest Pocket and the American DA. Were you to make holsters for these guns, this would be a great addition to your business, to the manufacturers, and to our catalog sales. To entice you, I would sell these eight pistols at our cost so you can start making the samples."

"Fantastic idea, if we were to order them thru our local gun shop, it could take weeks. We'll take them with us and start working on building the prototypes and send you a sample of each. If you approve, send us a telegram and we'll start manufacturing 50 of each holster."

"Well then, let me get my secretary to collect each firearm and prepare a contract as well as a bill of sale for the firearms and the 18 holsters/accessories. Meanwhile, let me give you a tour of our warehouse. I want you to see how your holsters will be categorized."

Walking thru the warehouse was an unbelievable sight. Every product on the catalog was in bins or on a pallet. Winston was explaining each section, but when we got to the ladies' dresses, Amy slowed her walk to a crawl. That is when Winston explained the mail order system.

"When an order comes in, a worker takes a wagon and two clip- boards. Note the number on that bin that has several dresses. The number is 1012-0089-029-12-5. This means 1012 is the vendor's number, 0089 would be the bin number, 029 is that blue dress, 12 is the size, and 5 is the number requested on the order. Now if the bin is getting low, the worker adds the entire number to the second clipboard, and the number will go to the reordering department. The five dresses are added to the wagon. Then to shipping with the completed order."

"Wow, who designed this system?"

"That was Aaron, our founder, and it has not failed us for years. Let's take one of your holsters as an example. 1007 would be your vendor number, 0718 would be the bin number, 018 would be the gunfighter holster, 002 would be the deluxe model, and 003 would be the 4 ¾-inch barrel length. Now you see why I am keeping your 18 holsters and why I want the next 8 ASAP so we can assign numbers and bins. The longest process is to make photographs and prepare a page of your holsters with all the descriptions, codes, and prices."

"As I understand, we have six months to ship you the original 900 holsters and the extra 400 for the other firearms you will be selling."

"Not quite, we wish your 1300 holsters as soon as you can manufacture them. We have many new vendors to process in the next six months before the next Wish Book edition comes out."

Amy had been quiet but was absorbing all this information. Finally, she said, "my experienced staff can put these out in seven days since we are manufacturing 200 holsters daily. We will build these 8 new holsters and send them to you for approval. By the time your approval reaches us, the original 900 holsters will be on their way and the 400 will follow a week later."

"I couldn't have asked for a better response. Let's go back to the office and sign some papers."

The contract was a straight-forward document which was signed in duplicate by all three parties. The bill of sale showed the 8 firearms to cost $175 and the 18 holsters/accessories came to $124 with the discounts added in. Randy included a bank voucher for the $51 difference. Once business was completed Winston added, "my secretary will accompany you to the Grande Hotel. We have a suite that we reserve for VIP's and Montgomery Ward will treat you to one night's stay and dinner in their elegant restaurant—the Rainbow Room. I will be joining you at 7 PM with my wife, Eleanor."

Amy noticed a photograph of Winston and Eleanor on Winston's desk. Amy asked, "is this the kind of dress ladies wear in the Rainbow Room?"

"Yes, the city is in a high fashion craze. The dress with a high collar is gone and there is plenty of exposed shoulders or décolletage in today's fashion. See you tonight, my secretary will make reservations."

After the duo got to their room, they were

amazed at the luxury. A two-room suite with sitting room, bedroom and a water closet/tub with hot water. The one item that was new was a rope attached to a piping system that rang a bell at the bellhop's desk. By pulling the rope a few times, a messenger would come to the room to inquire the occupant's needs.

Randy and Amy had arranged for some coffee to be delivered and they sat in the settee to talk. Randy began, "that was a major promise you made to Winston. Considering we are already behind with mounting back orders; how do you propose to put this MW order out and cut down our back orders?"

"I have been thinking about this for some time. It's going to be over a month for our second shop to be productive with new employees. We have to go with the experienced workers we have to catch up. We are six weeks away from the Christmas holiday. Harvey tells me that many workers are asking if they could do some extra work to cover the Christmas expenses. I think we offer everyone to work six or seven days a week till the holidays. If we're lucky, everyone will want seven days a week. Either way, these new holsters need to be produced by our present staff and not the new employees. What do you think?"

"I agree that our workers would welcome the extra wages. This means 'time and a half.'"

"I know, but we have spent several years building a reputation of a timely business, and I hate to see this situation chip at our reputation."

"You're right, let's do it. Now, I think we need to change for our dinner engagement." Randy changed in his three-piece suit and included his shoulder holster/Bulldog. Amy finally came out of the bedroom, and Randy nearly fell off his chair. "Ma'am, that is some plunging décolletage and a lot of skin. How come I never knew you had all 'that.'"

"Standing nude in front of you, well, everything sags. Now this dress has some new uplifting bands and along with the open chest exposure, this is what you get, heh. Expect Mrs. Ward to have the same type of dress, and she has twice the bosom I have. So, try to keep your eyes on me before you get in trouble."

Making their entrance to the Rainbow Room, the Wards were waiting for them in the foyer. After introductions were made, Randy had a tough time not looking at Eleanor's massive headlights, but Amy's pinches and kicks kept him in reasonable control.

Before dinner, the men had Scotch whiskey and the ladies had some red wine. Dinner was prime rib with all the fixings as well as a flaming caramel dish for dessert. During dinner, Amy noticed a patron who kept looking at her with a salacious and furtive look. After dinner the ladies excused themselves to go freshen up.

Amy used the water closet first. When done, Eleanor was next.

As Amy was touching up her rouge, suddenly a man stepped into the ladies' room holding a knife. "Honey, you're coming with me, we're going to have fun." Eleanor chimed out, "Amy is that a man in our bathroom?" The knife holding miscreant simply pushed the water closet door open. Eleanor's mouth was gaping open as she was seen holding her petticoats up while taking care of business. The man pulled his fist back, punched her in the face, and knocked her out.

As the man was busy with Eleanor, Amy inserted her hand in her reticule. The threat then moved to Amy, as the man placed the knife to Amy's throat, again repeating that they were going upstairs to his room. Amy never hesitated as she pulled the trigger. The loud blast pushed the bullet thru the base of the reticule and perforated the top of the man's boot top. The man fell to the floor like a rock in water. The screaming was enough to alert everyone in the restaurant.

Knowing that the gun shot would bring an army of people in the ladies' room, Amy rushed to pull up Eleanor's undergarments and pull down her dress. As expected, four men entered, Randy, Winston, the restaurant manager and the hotel manager. Randy was about to ask Amy what transpired when he noticed that the base of Amy's reticule was on fire. After putting out the fire and getting an explanation of events, Winston went to attend to Eleanor who was just becoming alert. Randy went to the moaning man and said, "does it really hurt that much?"

"Of course, get me a doctor."

"Well before we do that, we need to pull your boot off and stop the bleeding." As Randy, not too gently, yanked the boot off. The man just about passed out. To make it worse, Randy was examining the foot and happened to squeeze it without warning. This time the would-be kidnapper said, "Someday, I will kill you and that woman."

The hotel manager then said, "this man is a wealthy businessman who comes to the city on a regular basis. Every time he is here, some sexual crime occurs, and some innocent woman is raped. Now we have enough proof to put him in prison for some time. I'm sure the police will be happy to pick him up."

With the evening coming to an end, the Wards said their goodbyes. The duo headed upstairs to their suite. Randy was watching Amy undress as he said, "I'd forgotten how beautiful you are, and how we have missed so many opportunities to be intimate."

"Well, you know how busy we are with our businesses and how exhausted we are when we get home. Plus, we've had to abstain or you've needed to be careful in midcycle to avoid pregnancy."

"Well, tonight we are not tired, stressed, or need to be careful."

"But I am in mid cycle."

"There will never be a perfect time to raise our family. When we're young, it's as close to the perfect time. The business will always be there. So, I'm going to make love to you all night and not be careful, heh!"

The next morning, after a replenishing breakfast, the duo proceeded to the Central Police Station to file charges for aggravated assault and attempted kidnapping for nefarious reasons. Upon arrival, the officer asked the duo to step to the cell and speak to Mr. Walter Jenkins, the claimed assailant.

Jenkins came up to the bars and said, "I'm a wealthy man, and if you don't file charges, I'll give you $5,000."

"Does that cover the threat of killing us as well?"

"Ok, I'll make that $7,000 and you'll never see me again."

Amy responded, "when you had that knife on my throat, I had two choices. One was to shoot you in the groin and amputate your manhood and nuts—that would make you safe for all the women on earth. The second was to shoot you in the foot and send you to prison. I took the latter, and you need a prison term to expose you for what you are. Plus, maybe you'll get raped in prison which would really be justice, heh. If you ever come back to attack us again, I will shoot you in the groin."

After filling out all the papers, the officer said that the trial would be in two days and the prosecutor would definitely call on Amy and Eleanor as witnesses. That meant that Amy had today and tomorrow to shop and would likely fill an entire railroad boxed pallet with clothing and more.

True to form Amy had a mission. The work clothes, dresses and accessories were mounting up. Randy didn't mind it since he had a relaxed wife every morning and night. Things turned to reality when Amy started collecting baby clothes, bassinet and other newborn accessories. So, Randy finally asked if she was pregnant.

"Well, I could be the way you have been ravaging me for days. Now, if the deed may be done, there is no reason to stop ravaging me, is there? I swear, the last days were as if we were newlyweds again. Promise me to continue your treatment when we get home. That has to be the best incentive to maintain life as we know it, heh."

The trial lasted three hours. Jenkins attorneys tried to discredit Amy as a harlot who had asked for the attention. When all failed, the jury deliberated one hour and found Jenkins guilty on all counts. The judge then passed sentence and sent him to the Illinois penitentiary for five years without a chance for parole.

The next morning, the duo took the train back to Amarillo. The eight guns were in the luggage at their side, and Amy's purchases were in the freight car. Amy was going back to manufacture the eight holster prototypes, as Randy was supervising the construction of the second shop. Along all this hubbub, Cliff was building the derrick on lot #2. Fortunately, well #1 was still producing 72 barrels of oil per day. A fourth purchase of 5,000 barrels of crude from the same starting refinery gave Randy some room in the storage shed and gave him the extra $10,000 to help finance the new shop construction, new employees and a new oil well.

Meanwhile, Mr. Harper had been judiciously handing out donations. He presented his ledger of names and specific payments. It had totaled $1150 in the first month as expected to clear up old accounts. Randy especially like to see shotguns/ammo handed out—for it was better to show someone how to feed themselves compared to unlimited handouts. Mr. Harper was asked to continue his administration and management of the anonymous McWain benefactor fund.

**

CHAPTER 15

BEGINNING THE 20TH CENTURY

Arriving at the shop, the construction had gone well. The walls were up, and the crew was working on the rafters. Harvey had been working on advertising for new workers and put a stop to the initial screening interviews once he reached forty applicants that he had chosen to present to Amy. Amy decided to hold off the interviews till the eight holsters were finished and sent to Winston Ward.

The day before the interviews were to start, the owner of the shoe and boot shop next door came to see Amy. "Mrs. McWain, I'm closing my shop and moving to Houston. The parent company is forcing the move. They have more modern equipment that uses a right and left "lasts" that generates a right and left boot. We have been producing a single universal shoe that molds to the wearer's foot to generate the right and left boot. It would cost more to retool my shop than to incorporate my crew into the Houston shop."

"Interesting, but how does that affect my shop?"

"I have 50 employees but only 25 are willing to move to Houston.

That leaves 25 good leather workers who have families and roots to this community and will be looking for work."

"Now I am really interested, I will interview all 25 of those workers today. But before I do, let's compare the wages we are offering." Amy admitted that her workers were now making anywhere from $1.75 to $3 a day—depending on longevity and skills. After a careful analysis, it was clear that most workers would end up with a $10 increase per month and the opportunity to climb in stature and grade in a new company.

The interviews were held that afternoon and all 25 men and women were hired on the spot. While the shop's construction was in progress, all the new workers were assigned a position on the assembly line and were to work with their experienced instructors till they were able to take over the stage with the experienced person watching over them. When the shop was completed and all the new equipment powered up to the steam engine, the workers were able to move to their new assembly line.

Three weeks from the time concrete was poured, the new shop was in full operation. It was also a time for administrative changes. Harvey finally retired and the two shop managers, Eric Greenwood and Ray Harrison became the foreman of each shop. Melinda finally got a permanent assistant, and both worked together to cover both shops. Stella and Suzanne gave their six-month notice and would start training their replacements immediately to cover the inspection, filling orders and packing for shipping. Romeo also gave a tentative notice of retiring in the near future after he had trained two older men to take over his job. All four retirees agreed to come back when needed to replace sick workers or even during crunching times.

Amy became the master designer who was responsible for adding new items to keep up with the times. As the chief executive, she got involved with all decision-making issues, ordering of supplies, payroll and day to day problem solving. Melinda and her assistant worked in conjunction with Amy's needs.

Things were simply running smooth and back orders were finally being filled. Amy had gotten a whiff of a new handgun on the horizon. It was James Westland, her old employer, who told her of the new semiautomatic handgun, the Browning Model 1911. The military was bidding on replacing the Colt Peacemaker with this new handgun. Although, still in production and not yet available, Amy knew that this was the thing that could revolutionize the handgun industry. Amy asked James to get her a sample as soon as possible. Amy also sent a telegram to Chicago informing Winston of the current information and her request for a sample if he could get his hands on one. This was the first example where Amy needed to be on top of things to be prepared for a new product coming on the market. For her company to be successful, a new handgun needed a new holster and McWain Holsters should be making it right from the get-go.

Waiting for the next Wish Book edition was like the calm before the storm. Fortunately, McWain Holsters had the financial ability to continue making and storing holsters till the first order from Montgomery Ward arrived.

***

With all the activity at the holster factory, Randy was also watching over Cliff. The Tilton Company had already dug a water well and installed a windmill pump. The derrick was half built, and Cliff was again setting up for rotary drilling. Randy needed questions answered before he made other plans.

"Should I arrange for the storage shed to be built before the well comes in?"

"The odds are very high that this well will feed off the same reservoir, but until the well comes in, it's not here. Besides, if we get a monster gusher, the storage shed will be a mess and very expensive to clean. I suggest you wait."

"Should I order wooden oil barrels or wait for the steel ones to come out?"

"I think the steel oil barrels are still five years away. When they do, they'll likely be manufactured by Standard Oil or Humble Oil and may not be available for years to 'wildcatters' like yourself. As you did with your first well, have the barrel maker hold your order pending the well coming in. When it comes in, your barrels will be on their way. Until they get here, you have a reserve in your sheds that you can use."

"If and when we hit oil on well #2, how will this affect production in well #1.

"It could have no affect at all, but I doubt it. More than likely, the reservoir on well #1 is the same as well #2. In that case the primary pressure in well #1 will drop and equilibrate with well #2."

"So theoretically, the current yield of well #1 at 72 barrels a day could drop to 50 barrels and be the same as well #2.

"Yes, theoretically. But oil wells are so unpredictable that one has to wait to see what would happen."

"My last question is a bit confusing to me. At what point do you add a walking beam pumpjack, or a nodding donkey as you call it. Also, please explain, again, how this contraption works!"

"This pumpjack is powered by a steam engine which converts pressure to a horizontal shaft that turns a concentric wheel. The wheel lifts and lowers the walking beam which is pivoting on a Sampson post. The outer end of the beam lifts a sucker rod which removes oil from the well. When you see it in action, you'll realize how simple it is."

"Now the biggest question in the oil business is when to install this oil lifting equipment. The standard answer is to only consider it when your well is producing less than 50 barrels a day but more than 15. Anything less than 15 barrels a day is called a 'stripper well' and that definitely means you need a pumpjack to maintain a profitable margin."

"I can install a pumpjack and guarantee 50 barrels a day with the technology we have today."

"How do you decide when to add a pumpjack?"

"DEMAND, DEMAND AND DEMAND. If your shed is full of oil barrels and there is no demand, or the barrel price is low, it's not the time to add a 'nodding donkey.' You can always shut down the well. Crude oil won't go bad and with no oil wells within miles, it's not going to disappear. When the demand or barrel price pick up, we reactivate the well. Worse scenario, with two nodding donkeys, we can maintain production at 50 barrels a day per well. 100 barrels at $1.50 a barrel is theoretically over $50,000 a year. So, when the demand finally matches the supply, it will be because of the combustion engine requiring gasoline as well as a use for the other products of crude oil distillation."

"Should I order some pumpjacks ahead of time, to have them here ready for installation?"

"No, the technology is changing so fast that I would wait a bit longer. You have been lucky to have sold four large batches of 42- gallon oil barrels to independent refineries, and I suspect that this will continue. The refineries are storing and hoarding the refined products until the demand catches up. In order to continue hoarding, they will buy more crude oil from you since they can't get it from the oil giants who are hoarding their own crude oil."

"Very good. How long before you start drilling #2?"

"One week."

***

With time to spare, Randy decided to go back to the shop. Meeting with Amy, he asked how he could help since there was only waiting at the dig site.

"Yes, we need to rethink our shipping boxes. Our standard has been to send an order of several holsters to one merchant and place the holsters loosely in a large cardboard box. This is not going to work with Montgomery Ward. When we send an order, each holster will need to be placed in its individual box. Then each ordered model of 25 holsters will be placed in their own cardboard box. The cardboard boxes will then be placed in the railroad's wooden crates."

"Unless I'm not understanding, we need an individual small and large holster box."

"Yes. Here is the largest of the small holsters, and this one is the largest of the large holsters. I am holding the 900 holsters till I get individual boxes. I have already sent a telegram to Winston and he approves whole heartedly. So, would you go to the 'Brown' box and paper company and place an emergency order?"

Arriving at Brown Box and Paper, Randy went to the customer service desk. Once he explained what he needed, the agent measured each holster and placed the exact dimensions on his work order. He did some math and said that it would take a certain size box to hold 25 small holster boxes and a larger one for the larger holsters. When he was finished the work order he asked, "what kind of cardboard do you want?"

"What do you recommend?"

"We have two cardboards. The paperboard is a thick paper stock that is a heavy pulp. This would be ideal and cheaper for the individual holster boxes. For the large boxes holding 25 individual holster boxes, I strongly recommend our corrugated cardboard which is three layers. An outside and inside heavy paper with ridging flutes in-between the two layers."

"Sounds just like what we want."

"How many do you want?"

"I needed yesterday an emergency order of 1000 small holster, 1000 large holster and the large boxes that hold the 25 individual boxes. I will gladly pay for the immediate custom order. After that, triple the order and we'll reorder when necessary."

"Yes sir, let me check the availability with my foreman."

"The agent came back with the obvious foreman. For a special extra fee of $50 we'll have this order ready in three days and deliver it to your shop."

"Deal. Thank you."

That evening, after dinner, Amy asked how their holsters would get to the customers who ordered them from Montgomery Ward.

"When you were in the ladies' room with Eleanor, I asked that same question to Winston. He said that the way it is today, the individual customers receive their order at the local post office. It is up to them to pick the order up there. If one lives in a small town without a post office, the customer needs to set up an arrangement with an express or freight company to bring in their mail. Now in just a few years, rural free delivery or RFD will be enacted but it will take years for the system to be up and running."

"Since we're on the subject, do you know where and to who they ship 3 million catalogs?"

"Again, during our tour when you were involved in touching every dress in the bins, Winston answered that question. They send catalogs to general stores, mercantiles, gun shops, hardware stores, clothing stores, farm implements stores, stove shops, furniture stores, dry goods/grocery stores, jewelry stores and so many more merchant locations. Now you'll never believe who is their biggest customer."

"No idea."

"The private customers who have put sizable orders in the past year. However, he did not quantify 'sizable.'"

"It's inconceivable to imagine a mail order catalog serving the entire country. How can they do it?"

"Chicago is 1000 miles to Massachusetts, Georgia/Florida border, northern Texas and Seattle. That covers 80% of the country. They use the railroad to get packages to the major areas and then the postal service to local communities. They have the track record to prove it can be done at a profit."

"Hearing of a competitor by the name of Sears Roebuck adding their mail order catalog, do you think we'll apply to be a vendor?"

"This mail order thing is new to us. I think we need to see how it works before we spread out. Besides, with a competitor in the works, we may only be offered restrictive contracts. Time will tell."

"Well as soon as the cardboard boxes arrive, we'll send the order on it way. Afterwards, my goal is to build a massive inventory of all our holsters. I'm presently having Ed Learman build me some very large bins on wheels. I will end up with a bin for each holster which will make preparing shipments much easier."

"Never forget what Harvey told us years ago. Holsters are not like bread; they last for years. It is a bit frightening to think that the shop will soon be manufacturing 350--400 holsters per day. That means, we always need new customers, but more important, we need to make holsters for new handguns that come on the market. That's how you guarantee a market for your product."

Amy added, "and I suspect that we'll be advertising in many mail order catalogs in the future. I really believe that this will be the major advertising avenue as we enter the 20th century, heh. Plus, a population of +- 65 million is a reassuring customer base."

***

For days, the drilling continued without any evidence of oil staining the rock chips. When Cliff reached 185 feet, chips finally changed. Amy started coming to the drill site with Randy. As before, the washings eventually came up with crude oil. Without warning the earth shook and a roaring noise was heard. This time, Amy opened two large heavy-duty umbrellas to cover themselves from dripping crude oil.

The gusher exploded above the derrick pushing the rods and drill bits into the sky as a projectile that landed far away from the well. Crude oil was raining over everything and everyone. This time Cliff was able to cap the spewing well within 6 hours of erupting, making the mess much easier to clean up.

And so, the process began for the second time:

1. A steam engine was set up to clean the derrick, rigging, and surrounding well area.
2. The barrel company was notified, and barrels started arriving.
3. Ed Learman arrived with the posts and beams for the storage shed.
4. Maitland activated his crew and after setting up the pipes, pressure gauges and valves, determined that the yield would be 50 barrels a day.

During this extended preparatory period, another independent refinery was coming online. The giants wanted $2.50 a barrel and were not eager to sell to independents since they were supplying their own refineries. Randy offered them the usual $2 a barrel with paid up freight to the railroad depot. The deal was made and freight wagons carrying 8 barrels were making each three-mile run in two hours-time, or four trips a day. With four wagons in use, they managed 128 barrels a day.

The sale of 7,000 oil barrels allowed Randy

to pay all his expenses in drilling the well, buying barrels and building a storage shed. The original well #1 had dropped its production to 50 barrels a day to match well #2. The balancing oil production was as Cliff had predicted.

That morning, during a replenishing breakfast, Amy said to Randy, "Now that you are producing 100 barrels a day with all expenses paid, I would safely say that you are an 'oil man.' That has to be a person's life achievement, heh!"

"NO, I won't be satisfied till two more things happen."

"What are they?"

"Montgomery Ward mail order scheme becomes reality. This could guarantee the survival of McWain Holsters for our generation and the next one."

"What is the second?"

"Children, our family. More important than oil or holsters."

Amy came up to Randy, put both hands behind his neck and whispered, "you can check #2 off, as of yesterday and Doc Cavanaugh, we are pregnant."

Randy just held his wife and started tearing up. Amy knew Randy's caressing was his way of expressing his joy. Amy then added, "you had better brace yourself Mr. McWain. Unless the Doc has been drinking, he believes I'm carrying twins."

"What, how far along are you?"

"About three months."

"And you were so active last night during our lovemaking. Aren't we supposed to be abstaining or at least be less aggressive?"

"Nothing of the sort, Doc says life continues as usual which includes sex and work. Twins or no twins. When my heaviness becomes tiring or bothersome is when I'll change my routine."

Weeks marched on when Amy says to Randy, "the shop has now filled 24 bins, one for each holster. Each bin holds 250 holsters and so we have an inventory of 6,000 holsters. Today we are manufacturing the two new deluxe models, the buscadero and gunfighter rigs, and starting bin #25 and #26. My point is, since we've heard nothing from Winston Ward, have I made an error in building such a large inventory?"

"Now Amy, you're thinking of the old adage, 'in business, if you don't make mistakes, you're not aggressive enough.' Now, I don't think this was a mistake, when the orders start coming in, you'll be glad to have this inventory as a backup."

"I guess you're right, especially when you think of a 65 million customer base."

The next day, the post office delivered a special package. Amy opened the box and found the recently released edition of the Ward's Wish Book. The duo quickly opened the page to the firearms and holsters section. McWain Holsters had a beautiful two-page layout of their photographed holsters. Each holster had a detailed description of its attributes and details. The prices and ordering codes were included. Throughout the day, the catalog was passed thru the four assembly lines. Every worker saw the advertisement and each one realized how this would guarantee their continued employment.

Within a week, a telegraph messenger arrived

in a huff with a telegram labeled 'immediate delivery.'

Randy received the messenger and read the telegram as Amy was in one of her frequent visits to the water closet.

> From: Winston Ward, c/o
>   Montgomery Ward
>   Chicago, Illinois
> To: McWain Holsters
> We have a keeper, your holsters have sold out STOP
> Need an emergency replacement order STOP
> How many can you send and when STOP
> RSVP Today. Winston

Amy hands a written note that must be sent now. The messenger was told to standby for an answer as she hands him $1 coin. Her answer read:

> I have an inventory of 6,500 holsters STOP

How many do you want of each
model STOP
Can ship by tomorrow AM, in
individual boxes STOP
RSVP Today. Amy

Thirty minutes later an answer came back:

200 each of the deluxe buscadero
and gunfighter rigs STOP
100 each of the other 24 standard
holsters STOP
Keep making them, expect an
avalanche of orders STOP
Will reorder soon.
Thanks, Winston

Randy looked at Amy and asked, "how on
earth can you pack 2,800 holsters in individual
boxes and get them to the railroad depot for
loading to boxcars overnight. It's 1PM and the
morning train leaves at 6AM."

"Watch me!"

Before Randy's eyes, he saw what good
workers can do. Eric, Ray, Melinda and

employee, Suzanne, Stella, and visiting Harvey all gathered around Amy. Amy explained the situation, before minutes tables were set out, pallets of unopened boxes appeared, two full assembly lines were shut down and each worker was assigned a bin and 100 unopened boxes. By 5PM, the crated orders were on the wagons heading to the railroad depot.

Standing on the loading dock watching her 2,800 holsters leave the shop she said, "remember what you once told me how we can spend a lifetime building a reputation and can lose it overnight with a bad decision? Well this is one bullet we dodged, heh."

Three days later, busy at making holsters, another emergency telegram arrived.

> Have received your order, nicely packed STOP
> Have already accounted for 80% of this order STOP
> Please repeat the order ASAP STOP

Enclosed is a voucher to cover the
last order STOP
Winston

***

Over the next months, Amy's pregnancy
proceeded without complications. To help Amy
with the management of the orders, Romeo,
Suzanne and Stella decided to delay their
retirement till the baby came. Harvey was also
back in the shop at reduced capacity, only to
prepare and be ready to take over Amy's job
once her time came.

Randy had finally found his niche in the
shop. It came to pass, that everyone realized
Randy knew how to do every employees' job
from dyeing leather to packing holsters. Randy,
although a rich oil man, never hesitated to take
over a sick employee's job. Randy would walk
the assembly lines and when he saw an employee
getting backed up, he would step in and help
out till the back log was caught up.

With the orders coming in regularly, it was
not rare to see employees pinch in after the

assembly lines closed at 5PM and stay to help boxing holsters—and no one ever asked for overtime pay. When Amy saw her inventory bins getting too low, Randy would announce that the shop would stay open the next Saturday and Sunday at "time and a half pay." Volunteers would be needed since the work weekend was not obligatory. However, during that weekend, all four assembly lines were fully operational, and no one ever complained.

Six weeks before her due date, Amy had to stay home because of the size of her abdomen. She needed her recliner and bed to deal with the heavy twins. Suzanne and Stella would not leave her alone at home and split their time by alternating their days in the shop or at home with Amy. Randy was spending long hours with Harvey to keep the shop going. Montgomery Ward wasn't letting up with their orders.

Orders with private gun shops were picking up as well. Come to find out, a gun shop owner explained. "The discounts I get dealing with a firearms salesman and dealing with McWain Holsters are greater than the savings from

Montgomery Ward. However, the savings with general mercantiles are with orders on Montgomery Ward without using a middleman salesman—the tricks of the industry."

One day, Melinda asked Randy if he ever wondered why we never ran out of supplies. Randy had to admit, "No idea, never even thought of it. All I know is that there are plenty of belt buckles, rivets, conchos and the many accessories."

"Yes, you're right, but what about leather, leather dyes, and let's not forget thread for our never stopping sewing machines!"

"Ok, I give up, how do you do it?"

"My new secretary spends every start of her day checking the inventory of everything we use. To guarantee our supply, she now uses several suppliers. The classic example, vegetable tanned leather we need for our holsters is getting hard to find. We now use four leather suppliers and have to frequently buy leather in massive orders. Our leather inventory is abundant because of wise purchasing."

As Amy's day approached, Suzanne and Stella

felt comfortable leaving their replacements take over the packaging and shipping department. They had gained so much experience with the Ward orders that they were comfortable taking over knowing that Melinda was always there to help them if necessary.

Finally, Amy started having false labors. Doctor Cavanaugh decided to hospitalize her during her last week. Randy never left her side unless Stella or Suzanne were there to replace him.

One day, coming back from dinner, Randy was not allowed back in Amy's room. Amy was in labor and men were not allowed with their wives. Surrounded by Suzanne, Stella, a nurse and Doc Cavanaugh, the delivery went smoothly and quickly. The boy was born first, and the girl came some three minutes later. When Randy was called in the room by the doctor, he saw his wife holding two babies, one in a blue blanket and one in a pink blanket. Randy later admitted he still had that image visible when he closed his eyes at night.

For the next six weeks, it was a full-time job

for Amy to nurse two very hungry six-pound babies. By six weeks, Amy could not satisfy the babies even if she had an abundance of milk, so Doc Cavanaugh started the babies on two feedings a day of rice cereal mixed with cow's milk.

Amy was given all the help she needed. Stella and Suzanne arrived at 6AM to prepare breakfast, clean the house, do laundry, help with the babies' baths, prepare lunch and dinner, pickup whatever groceries were needed, run errands around town and always be around to hold the babies.

At eight weeks, by pumping her breasts ahead of time, Amy was able to start returning to the shop. Both nanny/grandmothers were always in attendance. Amy was pleased to see how well the shop had functioned under Harvey's supervision. Harvey was now 75 years old and it was time for him to stay at home to help take care of his wife Angela who had been in failing health lately. On Harvey's last day, Amy organized a retirement party at the end of the day. Her greatest gift was to promise

Harvey to be there for him and Angela to the end of their days on this earth.

The party came to an end and the duo was ready to go home when Sheriff Gusfield arrived, setting off his horse he said, "sorry to give you this bad news, but there has been a prison breakout. Three men escaped and Walter Jenkins was one of them. Not to upset you, but while in prison he told many inmates how he would kill the both of you when he got out. You must recall that you sent him to prison on a kidnapping and rape attempt charge. I consider this a dangerous man and ask you to take precautions."

***

Meanwhile, Jenkins and his two cell mates were picked up by employees of Levi Birchard, attorney at law. Now sitting in his office, a change of clothes, Colt Peacemakers and Win 73 rifles were provided. Jenkins was handed $1000 in cash and three horses were waiting for them at the local livery. All three men had prepaid train tickets to cover the 850 miles to Amarillo.

"You did well Mr. Birchard. Everything went according to plan."

"It should be, you paid me $5,000 to arrange all this. The most expensive part was to bribe the prison guards. The balance of your expenses come to $1,200 which I will withdraw from your account. Now, I hope you can start over in a location far from here."

"I will, but first there is some business we need to take care of!"

***

Amy was alarmed and said, "What are we to do? There is very little time, this animal could be here as quick as tomorrow if he can find the support that his money can buy."

Randy was not perturbed but knew he had to mount a protective ring around himself and his family. "Well Sheriff Gusfield, this character is a low life bottom feeder that preys on innocent women. He has now been exposed and will be out for revenge as he promised us. It seems to me that we can either run or stay put and wait for the predator to come to us, and he'll be coming."

Amy answered, "running is not a solution, it only puts off the inevitable. I say we wait for him, arm ourselves, and defend our family."

"Agree, but we need to stay together, that's not just you and me, but it includes the twins and the grandmothers. During the day, we'll all be at the shop and at night we'll be home. We will need a security detail and during my solo bounty hunting days, I made the acquaintance of a bounty hunter who has now retired and started a security agency. I hear that he has been successful, and I will wire him immediately. His main office is now outside of Denver and he can cover the 400 miles in half the time Jenkins can get here from Illinois."

Addressing Sheriff Gusfield, "while I'm at the telegraph office, would you gather James Westland, Maitland Annison, Ed Learman, Cliff Tilton and your deputies. I want to set up some protection till the security team arrives."

To: Cal Harnell
Harnell Security
Denver, CO
From: Randy McWain
Amarillo, TX
C/O An old member of Rainbow
Agency who guarded Clara
Family threatened by prison
escapee STOP
Need two 4-man teams by
tomorrow AM STOP
Include Max to guard twins.
Waiting for answer STOP

The answer came within a half hour:

Clarence Simpson and Omer
Westinghouse on way STOP
Each have three men. STOP
Will arrive by 9AM STOP
No charge for Max STOP
Stay safe—Cal STOP

When Randy returned to the shop, he
informed Sheriff Gusfield that eight men and

one dog would be here by 9AM. In response he said, "My deputies and I will guard the front and rear entrances to your shop till you go home. James, Ed, Maitland and Cliff will stay on guard at your home till tomorrow morning. I will return in AM before you open to check the shop and will stay on guard till your team arrives."

Amy was listening and finally said, "so we are all going to be together, either in the shop or at home with guards 24 hours a day. Now how can we safely ride thru town to get to the shop or home?"

Randy answered, "It's only three blocks or a five-minute ride. I will place men on business roof tops as protection, plus you and I will have rifles while riding thru, one rifle-armed security man riding shotgun next to the driver, and one on horseback. It's not a perfect defense, but it's the best I can come up with."

"It's almost overkill but am glad we can do it."

"It is overkill and for a reason. I want Jenkins and his buddies to realize that no matter how they attack us, bullets will be going back at them. These evil men are cowards. They will change their offense strategy and try to back shoot us. This will give us time to bring the fight to them."

So, how do you propose to accomplish this?"

"Tomorrow, after the Harnell agency arrives, the sheriff's deputies will visit every bar and diner in town. They will request that bartenders, waitresses, or merchants look out for three well-dressed men, one that limps, and all have short cropped hair—the mandatory prison haircut, heh. In return for notifying us, I'm offering a silent $200 reward.'

That afternoon, one of Jenkins toadies was sitting on the tonsorial shop's boardwalk when he noticed several armed men climb onto business roofs. Shortly thereafter, a well-armed carriage arrived with three women, several men and two babies. As soon as the carriage went by, the armed men came off the roofs.

That evening, Jenkins and another man were checking the woods surrounding the McWain house. The treeline was 150 yards away and thru an open corral for horses. One armed man was on the front and back porch, and one man was walking the tree-line while a second man was patrolling the front lawn and main road. After gathering this info, all three men met at McDougal's Saloon.

That evening, as the duo was getting ready for bed, a hullabaloo was going on outside. Clarence Simpson came to the door and said, "Randy, there is a messenger sent by the bartender at McDougal's Saloon. In the bar, are three well-dressed men, with the correct haircut, one man limping who has the top of his boot slit from ankle to toes."

"Bingo, we have them. Amy and I will go check them out."

Clarence added, "you need someone to watch the back and front doors. So, Homer and I are coming with you. I'll have four of my other men replace the four of us on the house guard duty by the time you're ready to go. Plus, Max stays next to the twins."

The duo armed themselves as was the custom during their bounty hunting days.

They both had their sawed-off shotgun on their backs and a Colt peacemaker at their sides. As they entered the saloon, Clarence and Homer immediately put their backs to the doors as Randy and Amy moseyed to the bar and asked for a beer. Confirming that their interesting party was at a table in the left corner, Randy stepped up to them, pulled out his cocked shotgun, and yelled, "you three men, stand up, and turn around to face me."

The entire room went as quiet as a tomb. Slowly, the three men stood up. Jenkins still had his back to the duo. As he turned around, Amy exclaimed, "what are you doing here, you're supposed to be in prison for years!"

"I came here to kill you, bitch!"

One of his toadies spoke up and said, "heh, we didn't bargain for a face to face gunfight with a sawed-off shotgun."

"Well boys, I'm not going back to prison, so when I draw on the bitch, you boys better draw against the shotgun, or you'll die for sure."

Amy interjected, "hold it Jenkins. Don't you

366 | Richard M Beloin MD

remember where I said I would shoot you the next time you threatened us?"

"Not worried, I'll outdraw you, you're not going to shoot me thru your reticule like you did last time."

Expecting an imminent gunfight Randy yells, "everyone, clear out of this room—NOW. As everyone was rushing out, Randy realized that Amy still had her shotgun in her backpack holster and was going to draw on Jenkins. So, he softly but with firm emphasis said, "Amy, this is not time for foolishness . . . . .Bang.

Amy was watching Jenkins eyes and pistol hand. As he blinked, his hand moved to the pistol. Jenkins had it almost out of the holster when a shot rang out. Jenkins bent over instantaneously as his pistol hand went to protect his manhood and jewels. The howl coming out of his mouth sounded like a wounded bear. At the same time, the two toadies had their hands up in the air. "Don't shoot, we give up."

After the shackles were applied, Randy reminded Amy that they needed to apply pressure to the wound or Jenkins could bleed to death.

"Well Randy, pull his britches down and I'll apply pressure to the bleeder."

Jenkins was totally oblivious. After the britches came off, Amy used her foot and stepped on the bleeder, at the same time happened to crush his one remaining nut. Well, Jenkins let go another wail to awaken the dead.

"Well, that won't work, heh. Jenkins, you'd better squeeze whatever is left of that little thing or you'll bleed to death. Nobody else in this room is going to touch your stub."

Clarence and Homer turned, and both had a smile from ear to ear. Homer was heard saying to Clarence, "I know a few philanderers that need 5 minutes with Amy for a permanent cure, ha, ha, ha."

Jenkins had emergency surgery that night, and the result according to Doc Cavanaugh was that this man would never rape a woman ever again and would have to squat to urinate.

Life continued and everyone was back to their routines. The shop was operating at full capacity. Amy found a new job. She became the quality assurance officer. A few mistakes had slipped in the bins, and Amy knew it was her responsibility to catch them before they were headed to customers. Every holster was visually examined and sent back to the worker who had made the error. Statistics finally showed that +-5% of holsters were returned to the assembly line. No one was criticized or had their pay docked. It was accepted as a natural occurrence when operating a shop at full capacity.

At the one-year birthdays, Randy shut down both wells since both sheds were full. With 12,000 barrels and the barrel price being down, there was no reason to increase the hoarding. One day, Randy had an idea which he shared with Maitland.

"We need to find a way to get the oil to the railroad yard cheaper than transporting it thru the teamsters and their freight wagons. Do you realize that it costs the refineries more to transport the oil barrels, for three miles, to the railroad yard than it costs to freight them by train some 350 miles to Dallas or even the 600 miles to Houston?"

"I think I have the answer. Have you realized when riding the three miles to the oil wells, that it is a gradual uphill ride. Plus, it is flat prairie land and only one road to cross. Let's get the three miles surveyed to see what the elevation exists between the rail yard and the well sites."

The answer came a week later. Both well sites were 110--119 feet above the railroad yard. Maitland then explained, "we need to order three pumps to supplement gravity since crude oil is sluggish. Plus, we'll have to purchase right-of-way to lay pipes on private property. It would have to be steel pipes above ground that can be inspected regularly. With pumps, crude oil will travel at 1.5 mph—or 2 hours to reach the railroad yards."

"Let's do it. I have no choice, with the market being down awaiting the Texas oil boom, I won't be able to move my oil. With a pipeline that knocks off a dollar per barrel, the refineries will be more eager to purchase my crude and allow me to reopen the wells. A pipeline is simply a method—it takes money to make money, heh."

And so, as the shop was keeping up with the orders, and his pipeline being installed, the duo saw their businesses flourish.

***

EPILOGUE

Over the years many hours were shared with the twins—Rebecca and Marc. By the time they were teenagers, they were already spending time with mom and dad at work. Rebecca had a gift with designing as Marc showed interests in mechanics and the oil business. Both kids went to business college and took a course with emphasis on artistic design for Rebecca and civil engineering for Marc. Both studies emphasized business management along with their chosen major.

During their school years in Denver, Amy signed a contract with Sears Roebuck similar to the one she had with Montgomery Ward. The biggest addition to their lineup of holsters was the 1911 semiauto pistol. It didn't take long for other semiauto pistols to follow suit. In addition, the double action revolver was getting refined and becoming popular. During the same time, Randy finally got his pipeline built. Right of way had not been an issue since the three landowners had been recipient of the McWain fund. A pipeline receiving plant, that refilled the wooden oil barrels, was built. When the steel oil barrel came on the market; the independent refineries were buying the oak wooden barrels at an obvious discount. They were being used to deliver the crude oil derivatives to customers.

As the 'gusher age" of the early 1900's came to an end, the roaring 20's brought a new era. Auto production exploded and the use of crude oil derivatives was finally in demand. Factories and industrial equipment were being powered by diesel engines, and homes were being heated with heating fuel. Randy's two wells were in continuous use and the barrels were filled at the railroad yard and automatically loaded on a side-railed boxcar. To speed transport thru the pipeline, two more pumps were added which kept the receiving plant at full operations.

During the twins' school years, they both married. Marc married a young lady who specialized in accounting and business office management. Rebecca married a man who had studied business marketing. Both twins and spouses managed to get employment in the Denver area. Now, in their mid-20's, the twins were encouraged to return to Amarillo and take over the two business. Mom and dad were ready to slow down, maybe do some traveling, or follow their hobbies.

When Marc arrived, his wife Gail was four months with child. Gail set up an office for McWain Oil close to the leather shop. Marc was given the go-ahead to drill for a third well on the remaining lot. Along with his responsibilities, he was given complete control of negotiations with oil refineries. Dad made it clear when he said, "this company is doing well when all wells are producing oil that leaves the plant at the railroad yard."

When Rebecca arrived, she was also pregnant and five months along. Her husband Ralph took over an idea he had developed a year ago. When he saw the books reflecting private and mail order catalog orders, he presented his idea to Rebecca and Amy. A McWAIN MAIL ORDER COMPANY. Rebecca was not surprised since she knew her husband's potential. Amy was a bit set back but said, "start working on this and keep me appraised. It has potential but you need to get Rebecca to come out with new products to make this shop a mail order company."

For the next month, Ralph and Rebecca worked together. Ralph was researching leather products at the library and Rebecca was designing standard and deluxe models of each item. At one time, they presented Amy a list of their current new additions:

- Extra-long ammo and shotgun slides
- Chaps
- Rifle and shotgun scabbards
- Derringer holsters, along suspenders or shoulder harness
- Developed a screw-knife to attach to any holster. The screwdriver portion fit the standard pistol screws

- Forearm cuffs to prevent rope burns
- Men's dress belts
- Leather suspenders
- Leather reticule
- Leather duffle bags
- 5 sizes of leather pouches, with or without belt loops
- Men's leather wallets
- Leather snake gaiters
- Backpack holsters for sawed-off or coach shotgun
- 3 sizes of saddle bags
- Balanced leather panniers to fit saddle without a packhorse and packsaddle

Amy looked at the list and smiled. "That's a good start and I haven't even added my suggestions. Well, Rebecca, you had better get to work making prototypes before the baby comes, heh."

Amy took Ralph under her wing and trained him to take over the business. Ralph was a conscientious and fast learner. Not only did he learn the old business, he also supervised the production of Rebecca's list of new items. Ralph never tired or objected.

Over the year, the orders from Sears-Roebuck and Montgomery Ward continued regularly which delayed the printing and mailing of the McWain Holster and Leather products' catalog. Ralph's brilliant idea was to mail batches of their magazines to every postmaster in Texas. The magazines were to be displayed as a free item for all to enjoy. The result was a shock to everyone. It was apparent that the Montgomery Ward and Sears-Roebuck catalogs had not reached everyone.

Over the years, Ralph kept the company thriving by sending another mailing to cover another state. Eventually, he started mailing magazine batches to east of the Mississippi. Several years later, he and Rebecca started adding sporting goods, guns, scopes, hunting knives, tents, camping supplies, fishing poles and of course holsters for the guns sold. Although the shop only continued manufacturing leather goods, a warehouse was built to house the many products arriving from many vendors. In a few years, they became a major mail-order catalog company.

Marc had managed to keep the pipeline working to their benefit. He was able to underbid many independent oil producers because the freight was so low. This meant that the oil wells were kept producing.

In time, as expected, the three wells had to have pumpjacks installed.

Years later, now in their 80's, the duo was sitting on their porch watching people drive by in automobiles. It was Randy who said, "do you even realize why our kids will save our companies for their next generation?"

"Well the answer doesn't come to me at this moment. However, knowing you as I have for some 65 years, I know you never ask a question that you don't already know the answer."

"Correct again, dear. How can we go wrong, we now have over a hundred million people that serve as our base for advertising our sporting products, and our oil. The demand is finally matching the supply, heh!"

Many generations later the McWain

Holster and Oil company names were changed to _____Sporting Goods and _____Oil Co.

***

THE END

Printed in the United States
By Bookmasters